KALEIDOSCOPE

KALEIDOSCOPE
TWO DAYS IN SPRING

VIVIENNE WOOLF

GAINSBOROUGH HOUSE PRESS

LONDON • CHICAGO, IL

First published in 2022 by Gainsborough House Press

Copyright © 2022 Vivienne Woolf

British Library Cataloguing in Publication Data:
An entry can be found on request

ISBN 978-1-909719-19-4 (Hardback)
ISBN 978-1-909719-20-0 (Paperback)
ISBN 978-1-909719-21-7 (Kindle)
ISBN 978-1-909719-22-4 (Ebook)

Library of Congress Cataloging in Publication Data:
An entry can be found on request

CONTENTS

MAINLY BLUE WITH SOME YELLOW

It is five o' clock on a Sunday afternoon in Bloomsbury. Scents of forsythia and hyacinth fill the air, daffodils and primula appear in gardens and house martins and swallows fly in from Africa to settle in London until the autumn.

In a clean and high-ceilinged third floor flat, Claire, whose life until now has been concerned mainly with tidiness and things money can buy, ends her day waiting for her only child, Lily to join her for supper.

Claire is sixty-six – not that you would know it, and attractive, if highly strung, with greying red hair and sapphire-blue eyes which are used to being admired. Now, after a night of interrupted sleep, but perfectly made-up, she hovers in a state of expectancy. She has studied her star sign, dusted her collections of porcelain birds and baskets, vacuumed the floral carpet, and bent over bowls of vegetables, peeling and seasoning them in preparation for the meal.

It's the time of year when London's squares are filling with a rising tide of life and people are celebrating longer days, sparkling trees, brighter colours and the promise that things might change for the better. But all this has the opposite effect on Claire. She feels tired and filled with the kind of late Sunday afternoon despair which makes some people long for Monday. Her thoughts take her back to the Sunday afternoon thirteen years ago when, in the grip of something dark and dreaded, she walked out of the life she shared with Lily and her father without a goodbye or warning, leaving Lily with only a pearl on a chain and a note.

Now, she traces a silk coil on the arm of her chair with her finger before looking out at the view across to St. Pancras and King's Cross Stations and at the late afternoon sky which reminds her, somehow, of lost opportunities, lost feelings, lost possibilities. While she is busy enough, she must admit that there are moments when her whole life – her whole difficult, ordinary life, feels like a dreary Sunday afternoon.

At the same time, but in a flat near Battersea Park, Lily is brushing her hair while the sun climbs down her bedroom wall. She is remembering the sounds of her parents arguing because nothing in her life has been sadder than her parents' divorce. Hairbrush in hand, she studies a photograph taken of her as a toddler, standing beside her parents in in a field somewhere. She can tell by looking at it that her father is a man of few words and that her mother is distracted but smiling, and she wonders – not for the first time – if the rift between them was caused by her.

Lily has been back in London for ten days and is looking for work – whatever she can find, having left the life she shared with her father, Marcus, in Cyprus, which had seemed a promising place, at first, but which soon turned into somewhere she couldn't fit in. And whenever Claire rang from London, she would tell Lily she was fine, fine even if she wasn't, or leave messages for her which didn't make sense.

Now, all Lily has left of her life on the island are photographs of her and Marcus sitting on beaches or posing in front of ancient sites or of Marcus wearing a cap and standing next to his pharmacy, pointing to his name, 'Marcus' on the sign.

Lily's flat belongs to her grandfather, Herbert, father to Claire and her half-sister, Sonya, and son of a man who became prosperous because he invented something. The flat is rooted in the family's history and is entangled in both past and present in a way Lily feels she is not. Although it is full of the quiet of a Sunday afternoon, when Lily opens a window, a voice offering hope drifts from the radio of her neighbour Sasha, a singer, breaking the silence and introducing the first movement of Mozart's clarinet concerto.

If Lily were to lean out of her window, she might spot a poet named Jonas, moving strands of hair away from his face, draped in a heavy coat despite the spring's warmth, and wondering whether to spend the night in his room or on a park bench.

And if she were to stretch out further, she might see Peter, her mother's lover, driving to his home from the garage where his late father worked, thinking that there is more traffic on the roads than usual. Peter has washed, polished and waxed his beloved brown Volvo in preparation for his visit to Claire, while picturing her beautiful hands which are young for her age, and which lure him like sirens towards her.

In the distance, but hidden from Lily's view, is the River Thames which winds its slow way through the city's excitement because rivers know that there is never any hurry.

From the outside Lily looks like an ordinary person watching life on the streets below but inside her, a life is beginning; she is newly pregnant, but has not shared this news with a soul.

If the late afternoon is dragging for Claire, she is used to waiting. She waits for days to end, for the rain to stop, for the phone to ring, and, in her dreams, for the existence beyond life on earth to begin. Almost all her life is about waiting. And how ironic it is, she thinks, that waiting, once the curse of earlier, unhappier days, should currently hold so much value.

Now, she is beginning to feel apprehensive. Her waiting is rising inside her like a tide. Ah well, so be it. At least this afternoon's waiting has a purpose; she is waiting for Lily and has pictured their reunion again and again till it has almost worn a groove in her thoughts. What difference does an afternoon make when she has been waiting for Lily for nearly two years? Her heart pounds as if she were waiting for a lover. She has changed from a plain skirt and blouse into a silk dress, belted and buttoned down the front, and is wearing black high-heeled shoes. Is she overdressed? Should she change back again? Should she have a cup of tea? Will she recognise her daughter? There are moments when anxiety overwhelms her, moments when she might be rearranging furniture, or watching seasons change, or in the middle of a wakeful night.

Be all this as it may, she looks around her room with pleasure; at the still-life paintings, porcelain ornaments, coffee table books, mainly blue upholstered chairs and sofas and the large windows overlooking the statue of Charles James Fox, a nineteenth century politician dressed for posterity as a Roman senator. She rises from her chair and caresses the curtains. Nothing has the power to comfort and care for her more effectively than this room, and she believes that if she waits in a room furnished as tastefully, all will be well.

She plans to tell her daughter she can never go back to the person she once was or the life she once led. She intends to turn things around and start anew; set right her wrongs. She hopes to listen to what Lily has to say. She wants so much to be a mother who spends less time worrying about what has happened, what might happen, or about being good enough or bad. But, notwithstanding her efforts, her grudge against Marcus remains.

Lily arrives at last, wearing Claire's pearl on a chain around her neck and carrying a bunch of daisies tied with a yellow ribbon. She is a force of nature and brings the spring evening with her like a trail of hope. She always made a point of being different, thinks Claire, always dressed differently from other girls.

Claire's brave smile is painted on her face. She admires the pearl, thinks how beautiful her daughter looks in her yellow trousers and has always loved the small gap between Lily's front teeth. Her daughter's hair is tied in a clasp, and she is wearing no make-up, but her skin glows as if she had finally passed from childhood into adulthood. And she remains polite, Claire observes with some satisfaction; in that respect, at least, Claire hasn't failed.

It saddens her to think that Lily may have built herself a world of memories in which her mother is nowhere to be found. Still, if Lily imagines that she is unlike her in every way, she is wrong. There is no mistaking her for Claire's daughter; she has Claire's curly hair, her skin, which is as pale as paper, and the same look of surprise in her eyes.

'You came,' Claire says, 'I've waited so long for this moment and have imagined it so many times. It can't be easy for you to walk into my flat.' She smiles as she speaks, takes Lily's daisies and puts them in a jug. Then she stands like a slender question mark in front of a large vase of spring flowers, which seem gaudy by comparison, filling with their scent a room which has remained unaltered over the years because Claire finds change uncomfortable. She prays Lily doesn't notice her too tight dress and wonders if her daughter realises how much the passage of time has altered her; she has aged, and there are days when her face doesn't seem to belong to her anymore. At least Lily can't hear what she is thinking or at least she hopes she can't.

She watches Lily walk slowly towards her as if crossing the distance of the life she has lived away from her. Did she experience enough of Marcus's world where Claire imagines everything was black-and-white or right-and-wrong to decide she had no part in it?

Claire is lost for words, chasing an emotion she can't quite name. Still, it's enough to see Lily sparkle in the sunlight which shines across the floor. Claire keeps on smiling, wondering if nearly two years was long enough to turn Lily into a stranger. She would like to tell her how often she tried to visit her in Cyprus but was prevented from so doing because Marcus had sole custody, not to mention the fact that he feared for his reputation. At least he is discreet, she thinks, he is that sort of man.

'Lily are you ok?' she asks, regaining her composure, and trying to suppress the uncomfortable sense that something she can't quite put her finger on is wrong. It might be better not to know, she thinks.

'Why do you ask?' Lily replies, rearranging her hair clasp.

'I want to know that everything's in place. I have an extra sense about you. Always have had,' Claire replies. 'Come here, come here, come towards me. You've gained a little weight and you're full of light. Looking at you is like looking at the sun; the sun would be envious of your light.'

Lily's light fills Claire with unexpected longing, reminding her of places and times long past. She can almost taste Lily's light and wonders if other people can see it – and taste it, too. But she fears that the sun might be closer to her daughter than she will ever be. She closes her eyes then opens them and says, 'Come and sit beside me. I hope nothing is wrong.'

'Oh Claire, what can I say?' answers Lily.

Claire's dress is the exact blue of her eyes, and she has pinned a white crystal bow brooch to her right shoulder like a medal. Blue suits her and she knows it. She is sticking with blue. She embraces Lily then holds her back in order to study her elusive features and marvel at her hair, which is still so bright yellow, it stops people in their tracks. Lily was a beautiful baby and is still beautiful. There is a luminescence to her. Does Claire envy her? Perish the thought. There are invisible threads which bind them. They always will.

'How are you? How are you?' she twice asks, 'I am so glad to see you. You've cheered my Sunday; Sundays often make me feel a little blue. I love the light which surrounds you. I have to stop myself seeing you as the little girl who brought me bottles of sunshine so I could plant trees like the trees which grew in the garden of my childhood.'

She takes a seat by the table, folding her arms on it and resting her chin on them. Everything is in its proper place. Everything waits. Nothing gets moved or changed. She stares – too long, perhaps – at Lily who is sitting forward in her chair with her legs crossed on its lower rung and with her hands on her stomach, caught up in thoughts Claire can't begin to guess and avoiding eye contact.

'You remind me of my father,' Claire says.

Then she rises, steps away from her child and, as if summoned by them and as if putting right a wrong, rearranges the vase of spring flowers which are so majestic she almost curtsies. Behind the flowers are two photographs: one of eleven-year-old Lily looking hopeful – the first time Claire realised she was beautiful – and another of Claire and Marcus looking glamorous but expressionless on their wedding day.

Claire looks at the wedding photograph then, from the corner of her eye, sees Lily watching her, so she summons up courage and says, 'There was a time when your father and I moved to music and didn't care what anyone thought, but The Blues we were hearing turned out not to be the same. The sun stopped shining for me and I went to a scary place where my family could predict nothing about me except that I would be someone they had never met before each time they came across me. But this was a long time ago – thirteen years to be exact – and I have changed. Age has helped me. I accept. I wait. Yes, I wait.'

She carries on talking but wishes she could stop. Then she removes a leaf which has fallen to the carpet; her desire for perfection, for bringing order to life's chaos, remaining paramount. When she tosses the leaf out of the window, she sees a complicated kaleidoscope of colour; London's glimmering lights, then, reflected in the glass, Lily's face and – her eyes may be deceiving her – she is looking at herself.

She returns to her seat, smiling, trying to appear as hospitable as possible and to hide the fact that she has remained anxious over the years. She wonders if Lily is hungry.

'Are you hungry?' she asks. 'Will you have something to eat? Something simple?'

There is silence. The scent of hyacinths infuses the room.

Lily isn't hungry, but says, 'Ok.'

Claire pats the seat next to hers. 'Move closer.'

They position themselves under an oil painting of a dead pheasant, placed on a tray together with a carafe of wine and a bowl of cherries. On the table before them are glasses which sparkle, plain plates and patterned plates, some given to Claire by Herbert, and all neatly positioned on a damask cloth next to napkins folded like roses because table arrangement is important to Claire. Her attention turns to the cucumber soup, cold roast chicken, tomato salad, bread, asparagus quiche, a bowl of green apples and bottles of water and wine. They help themselves. Claire fingers her wine glass, then pours herself water. She serves Lily wine, talking at first of matters outside her control, like weather and the lives of people whose names Lily has never heard. Then she touches Lily's arm before raising her glass and calling out, 'Cheers! Good health. Let's drink a toast; the toast is us.' She smiles at the room.

'I waited once,' says Lily, 'After you left us, I waited for you to return. Your departure left me feeling alone and unloved and unimportant. I would have loved having you around all those years. I trusted you because I had no choice, but you didn't bring me up.'

Claire doesn't say anything. She can't answer. She isn't prepared for this.

Instead, she touches her daughter's arm again, 'I've been longing to ask; what did you do out there? With your father? Has he found someone else? Remarried, I mean?'

Claire wants to know whether the Lily she knows is the same as the Lily Marcus knows. What did he tell her about their divorce? Is he closer to her daughter than she will ever be? Might he return to London and take Lily back?

When Lily doesn't reply she asks again in a small and unfamiliar voice, 'I want to know that you were alright. Were you? Are you?'

Lily and Claire look at each other across a void then Lily answers, 'I could tell you that I'm alright but instead, I'll say that I am sad. What do you expect?' She then sees the expression on Claire's face and says, 'I'm sorry,' but she says this as if she were speaking to herself and her voice is so soft that Claire is forced to ask, 'Say again?'

They then go on to talk about Lily's childhood which was different from that of other girls; Claire was often absent, and Lily didn't have close friends the way other girls did. 'Time seemed to drag then,' says Claire. 'Now, time passes like speeding cars. I'd give anything to slow it down, to make up for lost opportunities.' She leans towards Lily, closes her eyes and adds, 'I wish I could have lived without making wrong turns. Without anxiety. Without hurting or being hurt. But I have learned that is impossible. Was your father nice to you? Did he ever mention me?' She opens her eyes.

Lily says nothing and her silence unnerves Claire who asks 'Quiche? Soup? Salad?' feeling a little wild now. She accentuates each word as if it were a separate entity, but this only serves to make her feel more out of control and to wonder what she is doing. It would be easier to scream.

'Forgive me. I am so nervous; I am talking too much. I haven't given you a chance,' she says, 'What are you thinking?'

'Nothing,' is Lily's answer.

Claire is taken aback. Lily must be used to her missteps, she thinks, and to be covering for them, but this is hard work for her. Can Lily notice the dark circles under her eyes? Perish the thought, but is that a shadow of pity crossing Lily's face?

The silence between them becomes so uncomfortable that Claire forces a desperate little laugh, which curls along the table.

'Are you happy to be back in London, Lily?' She sips her soup. What harm can a question like this do, she asks herself as she points with her spoon towards her daughter, wondering whether Lily's answer will be, 'I'm ok'.

She and Lily may well come to understand each other, she hopes. They may even do something ordinary together like go shopping.

Lily uncrosses her legs and says, 'I'm ok. I'll be fine.'

Then they both laugh, uneasily at first, but in a way only mother and daughter can. Claire is glad to be laughing with her daughter and at the same joke – whatever that is – because she is shy around Lily and because, for a moment, nothing else makes sense.

'I have often pictured our laughing together,' she says. 'Anyway, I can see that you're ok despite the twists and turns, the ups and downs. Would you like an apple?'

She helps herself to an apple, and when she puts the half-peeled fruit on to her plate, notices the untouched food on Lily's and sees that her daughter is walking away as the setting sun brushes her one last time, making patterns on her arms and face.

'Good God!' Claire exclaims, 'Is something wrong? Is it the food?' She thinks Lily is being unreasonable, at first, but then wonders if her daughter might be feeling a bit off-colour. She smiles her brave smile.

'No. Thank you for the meal,' Lily answers.

Claire watches the sun fold over Lily like a protective cloak. She watches Lily pause in its glow before setting off like the moving flower she is, blooming but rootless. Claire rises and walks to the door, where she stands for a moment before waving her hand over her head and calling out, 'Thank you for coming. Thank you for coming. I'm lucky to have you. Let's see each other again soon.' But her voice sounds high-pitched and artificial, even to her.

Did Lily hear all this? she wonders. It's so difficult saying goodbye when you've just said hello.

'I have no business being a mother. I behave clumsily and am too full of mistakes and imperfections,' she says out loud, as she scrapes Lily's untouched food into the bin, 'but Lily and I have to begin again somewhere.' She feels knocked back by an unexpected wash of emotion and a headache and can't remember when last she felt so unsettled by the feeling that things didn't turn out as she had hoped, and by the silence left behind after a guest's departure. It all ended too abruptly, she thinks, and wishes she had been left with something more. Her flat seems different in some way, too; everything remains in its place, of course, but the room seems less alive, the furniture seems crumpled, and the paintings skewed. She didn't say the things she planned to say, and her unasked questions lie wasted on the floor.

Her friend, Peter is due to arrive. She goes to her bedroom, takes a painkiller and reapplies her lipstick in front of a mirror. Then she touches a tissue to her lips and moves her tongue across her teeth.

The doorbell rings and rings again. She jumps.

Something is wrong, she thinks, then wonders why she always thinks something is wrong in the world when what may be troubling her is something in herself. She drinks a glass of water, re-checks her lipstick and runs to the door.

Lily makes her way home under a sky spread purple by the setting sun. She walks through Battersea Park and almost – but not quite – passes a bench which Jonas, the poet, calls his own.

When she comes to sit on the edge of her bed, she thinks about what was said and what was not said and about her place in it all, and she cries for her unhappy start in life and for the child beginning its growth inside her. She remains seated and unmoving for a while. Then she takes off her shoes, loosens the clasp from her hair and runs her fingers through her curls, turning to left and right in front of her dressing table mirror, trying to see what Claire saw. She studies her still-flat belly, which will soon be swelling like a ripening fruit, she presumes. She manages a smile, picturing herself as a singer, a dancer or an actress; someone free and wearing red lipstick or rising out of waves covered in seaweed and pearls; someone like her neighbour Sasha must be, she imagines, and as desirable.

She knows there will be changes in her life, just as she knows that the same sequence of days can arrange itself into several different stories, and that it's impossible to think of one story without taking account of the others.

PURPLE

While birds flutter around him, Jonas, a twenty-nine-year-old poet and wanderer, and a country boy who is growing old in the city sinks onto a park bench. The bench is hard and pitiless and seems to hold all the hopes and fears of anyone who has ever sat on it, but Jonas loves it because it expects nothing of him. It is carved with the words, 'For Olive, who loved the park.'

'Is my notebook still under the bench where I left it?' he asks the fluttering birds.

Jonas is a poet because he can't help himself, just as he didn't choose to be a wanderer; destiny chose this for him. And once destiny chooses you for a wanderer, you spend your life wandering. His parents are dead, and he has no family to fight for. Nobody knows where he comes from and, if his life is about secrets, he is keeping them. He has woken in strange beds and unknown rooms and there are days when he doesn't see the sun. For now, he is a citizen of everywhere and nowhere. Still, he sees his past life as part of his story about keeping going and he remembers gently sprinkling his foster mother's ashes over grass.

He wonders how he arrived at this bench. Things happened which should never have happened, things that now seem out of place and wrong. But at least the poetry he writes keeps the past from looming over him, darkening his days without warning as once it did. His poetry is full of colour and questioning and will take him to a better, happier, more connected place. Or so he hopes.

'I am single as London's only lighthouse. If everything is nothing, at least my feet are on the earth and my hands touch the sky.' Words travel through his mind and on to his page and his lips move at the same time as if he were in conversation with an invisible companion.

Battersea Park is turning chilly. Jonas pulls his cap over his curls and down to his eyes. He leans his head against the bench, looks at the clouds and sees faces and distant places.

'I pick bits of stories which are not my own and travel down roads which have nothing to do with me,' he tells the faces in the clouds.

Every road has been Jonas's home but, right now, when he is not on the bench, he lives alone in a room in social housing, which is seldom blessed by sunlight and stuffed so full of the newspapers he collects that he can barely find space to walk around it. 'I may not have a family, but at least I have my room,' he says.

He likes the solidity of his room, and its stained carpet inspires him with its bleakness. A single lightbulb dangles like a naked eye from a cord on the ceiling and the walls are blank, except for a photograph of a man sleeping near a bicycle which is propped against a tree. Jonas loves everything about the photograph, but, most of all, he loves his fanciful idea that the man seems to have a life full of possibility; he can cycle off anytime and anywhere. Jonas often gazes at the photograph until his vision blurs, and he often stays longer in his bed than he should, picturing the man rising, walking towards his bicycle and departing for another life. He likes the fact that God knows how many people have occupied his room before him, and he only moves from his room to the bench as a way of finding air and light, trees and sky.

Earlier today, he woke in his room to the sight of sunlight dangling in the dust on the carpet and to the sound of a pigeon tapping on his window – one, two, three – as if telling him to get out of bed and keep moving. He left his room wearing the same clothes he'd worn the day before, but not his coat. Best to tiptoe through Sunday, he thought, before returning to his room, pacing around and grabbing his coat because he felt like he had mislaid a portion of his life.

Now seated on his bench, he watches the last of the sun take its time. He sees it laying its gentle hands around tree trunks, drifting over the grass and on to two swans which appear on the pond with their feathers glowing. He closes his eyes and sees the lone figure of a boy waiting for his foster mother to fetch him from school. When he opens them, he wonders where he is; he is on a familiar bench, of course, his jeans are still the blue of evening sky, and his coat remains where he placed it. And there, under the bench – what a miracle – is the notebook he left behind a week ago. This is the notebook he tucks under his head when he sleeps because he can never be sure, and this is the notebook which holds his life and, he likes to hope, waits for and listens to him. In it, he writes about love and solitude, dark and light, and in it he writes about the woman he has made his muse; and that woman is Lily. Jonas hasn't met or spoken to Lily and doesn't know her name or where she lives, but, from the safety of his bench, he has watched her running through the park like a spring breeze. She and he are like stars separated from each other in the sky, he tells himself, and were they to meet, he would be full of dazzling brightness; he might even stop drifting.

For now, it is dark which comforts Jonas. Even as a child he preferred the night to the day. Darkness soothes and softens the city and when the dark lulls everyone else to sleep, the world is left to him. He doesn't like spring. He doesn't like walking through places where trees change, and spring seems to have come around early with its smiles, its blossoms, its relentless green and white and with bodies showing their pinkness.

Although weather plays little part in his story, if asked to choose, he would say that autumn is his season. London is both dark and alive and mellow in autumn, and he can remain in his room. If he must go out, there are fewer people on the streets. But now that it is spring, the world smells of hyacinths, the duck pond has thawed, and the wind sends blossoms rolling like snow down paths in the park. He accepts this. He presses his hands to his eyes and sees through his fingers, bits of sky and leaves. And there, curved over the trees, is a rainbow. A sign. And signs are important to him.

A poem forms in his mind. He opens his notebook and writes, 'I find meaning in a rainbow's light, in swans on a pond, gliding in the night, in a park turned amber by the setting sun, in solitude which is hard won...'

A small green butterfly lands on the bench and he again draws Lily into his thoughts because his desire for solitude mixes itself up with his need for love.

The Lily he imagines is full of a million different facets of light mixed with a little dark. He sees her everywhere and nowhere; for him, she is a symbol of redemption. He imagines their meeting under an oak tree and recognising in each other the same restlessness. There are times when he dreams of her stepping into his room as if she belonged there.

'You won't remember me,' he says to the Lily in his dreams as she removes her shoes and shakes her hair loose from a clasp. 'You won't remember me because you don't exist. You are the silence between words, the song which isn't heard. May I talk to someone I don't know?'

He asks this question of the trees and the sky as if they might provide the answers which he and Lily need to find between them.

BLUE AND BROWN

'How are you?' asks Peter when he walks into Claire's flat around ten o' clock on this Sunday night, carrying a box of chocolates. The Beatles' song 'I Want To Hold Your Hand' is running through his head giving the lie to the pain in his heart, and his bifocals hang from a chain around his neck. He has worry beads in his hands because he never feels quite himself without them. He takes off his shoes.

Claire surveys him with such unexpected warmth in her eyes that he feels a catch in his chest.

Peter met Claire when she spilled her soda over his trousers in a pub which they both frequented. He bought her another drink, then took her home and they've been together on and off for four years. Because he always dreamed of leaving his neighbourhood and buying or renting a flat such as Claire's, he says, 'Of all the places in London I love but can't afford, Bloomsbury is my favourite.'

Claire offers her face; Peter kisses the air beside it. Then he throws his jacket on to the table, rolls up his shirt sleeves and observes – not for the first time – that the shade of blue upholstery on the chairs is the same as the trousers he wore as a schoolboy.

'How sweet of you,' Claire says, taking the chocolates, her head still full of thoughts about Lily. 'Lovely chocolates – thank you. Thank you. I don't know how I am. I woke at three this morning and stayed awake till the sky was pale with light. Will you be here long?'

'I'll be here for a while if that's alright,' he says, settling into a soft hollow in one of the chairs. He stares at Claire. She is as impenetrable as she is beautiful. He would love to assume more importance in her world; he would love her to need him as much as he needs her. Apart from anything else, he sees her as his fragile strand of connection to civilized life.

He wants to put his arms around her but something about her prevents him, so he pauses for a moment before attempting to kiss her cheek again. Claire is looking beyond him as if searching for someone else. He is not one to notice much about a room and its contents but must admit, once again, that the shades of blue make an impact; even the carpet is pale blue, and he becomes aware that she matches – blends in with – the room. The question he tries not to ask is 'Why?' At the same time, he finds blue soothing; it is the colour of longing, after all.

Claire hates night visits but doesn't say so. Instead, she asks, 'How are you? You look well. You used to visit more often. Is something wrong?'

He wants to say, 'Nothing is wrong' or, at least, 'I don't know what's wrong', or 'I am fine', but things aren't always so fine.

'Did I used to visit more often? I am busier now. Who isn't busy? You? How are you treating life?'

Claire nods distractedly. 'I'm not sure what you mean,' she says.

Peter starts to explain.

Claire says, 'Don't worry.'

He looks at her long nails and delicate hands – hands for straightening his tie or ruffling his hair, hands which caught his attention in the first place, and which often come to him out of the blue, so unlike his mother's workaday hands. Spring breathes longing into a man, and he is attracted to Claire.

There is little need to go into what two people have confided to each other except to say that most of their conversations were in the past. Peter and Claire spoke about their childhoods, about the roads they travelled, the music they liked and the houses they lived in. Claire told Peter she loves dancing and that she met her ex-husband at a dance although, these days, she seldom dances.

'The world dissolved around me when I danced with him,' she said, 'It was when I danced with him that I felt free. But I don't dance anymore; I can live alone but I won't dance alone.'

Peter enjoys dancing as much as the next man but believes that even if two people dance the same dance, they feel differently. Everyone dances to their own tune, after all.

He turns away from watching her and wondering what she thinks of him, to stare at his tired reflection in a window. A seagull disappears into the darkening sky and the curtains billow in the breeze.

Both he and Claire live alone – they have that in common – and it may be that they are bound to each other by no more than past mistakes and lessons learnt. But when Claire asks, 'I wish I knew how to be around Lily. I don't know what to do about her. Would she be good enough if she turned out like me?' Peter can't help her.

'Don't you get tired of talking about her?' he asks.

'She's my daughter and I'd like to know what's going on in her life,' she replies, 'What's going on in yours?'

'This and that. Driving around,' he answers.

She knows me only as 'the younger man', he thinks. He is so tired he could kill someone. His left eye twitches like it does when he is stressed.

Then, he watches her pull from her hair the side combs which pick up the colour in her dress, and sees her greying red curls fall loose. He looks into her eyes. She pours wine for him and water for herself. They clink glasses and kiss, and she leaves a lipstick stain on his mouth which will seem important till something more important comes along.

'Hold me,' he says, 'Hold me in your arms.'

He takes his bifocals from around his neck, puts them on the table with his worry beads and unbuttons her silk dress as slowly and as gently as he can.

'I don't know what I would do without you. If you went away, you would be taking something of me with you. Think about it,' he says, and his awkward words stay in the air. They are like that.

'Oh Peter,' she says.

Now, she turns out the lights and they go to her bedroom, her thoughts, as always, on her daughter.

They make love like it has to last. Claire feels young again and as if she were dancing to the sounds of a rhythm guitar, strummed under a sky full of little green butterflies.

When their conversation stops and their questions remain unanswered, the flat is quiet, so quiet, Claire believes she can hear a petal drop. It is something to have ended the day without disaster, she thinks.

Peter falls asleep with her hands on his chest and the worry that his heart may not be able to sustain much more of this. Their story began in her bedroom and could easily end there. Still, it may well begin again. For now, at least, they are together.

PINK

Although they have not said much to each other beyond 'Sunny afternoon' or 'Cold evening', Sasha loves the radiance which surrounds her new neighbour, Lily. She watched Lily move into the building and is struck by the way Lily runs instead of walks, the way she appears to bring light just by being there, and the way she makes Sasha believe she is not as alone as she fears.

Sasha is a trained singer whose spirit needs to sing. She would like to have been named Alice because Alice seems to be such an English name, but she never got the chance to ask her mother why she called her Sasha. Sasha's eyes shine when she sings and her voice is pretty, but she sings less often in public than she would like. When she sings, her voice echoes the feelings in her soul. When she sings, she comes alive, she knows who she is. When she sings, her father, Darius's face beckons to her through the bars of her music. And when she sings, she thinks about her mother, Tatiana, who died when she was fourteen and whose name is tattooed on her wrist. She also thinks about Lithuania, the country of her parents' birth although she hasn't been there.

Sasha is small-boned, with a strawberry mark on her neck. She wears her straight, fine, dyed-pink hair pulled back from her face. Her hands are so tiny they are almost child's hands, but her nails are usually painted Carmine pink and her arms are surprisingly muscular from gardening, which is her hobby. She lives alone and has always felt herself to be an outsider. Still, she cheers herself by wearing floral dresses bought from vintage shops and has been told she has an old soul. She also has a talent for listening and accepts most people whatever their strengths or flaws.

Darius, her father, knew a great deal about cars and although he had played in the second violin section of an orchestra way back in time in Lithuania, he worked in London as a minicab driver. He often spoke about Lithuania and about why he left, and he kept hoping that he resembled an Englishman.

When Tatiana died, Sasha cried and asked Darius to explain tears. He said, 'Tears pass just as life passes and everyone dies eventually. While I know as surely as my name is Darius that all men and women must leave this earth, I am not, unfortunately, able to explain tears except to suggest that today's tears might fuel tomorrow's cars. You never know.'

Sasha nodded the way you do when an explanation is inadequate, but you accept it, anyway.

She asked, 'How do you know?'

'I don't know how I know,' was his reply, 'We just have to hope.'

When Sasha turned thirty, Darius used his savings to buy her a grey car before returning to Lithuania because as far as he was concerned, cars give the only freedom there is by getting a person from one place to another. 'That said, I can't stop feeling foreign in this city,' he added. 'Although I could listen to your singing for ever, things have changed. We need money. Refuse to give up. It's the best lesson I can teach you. Consider your life from a driver's perspective; there are always roads waiting to be explored. I expect to return to London a wealthier man.'

But he never told Sasha that he had no wish to die in a city which did not seem to need him and that, believer though he once was, he would be returning to Lithuania, an atheist.

'Dear Sasha,' he said as he walked out of the door, 'You are a woman now and people do this all the time.'

'Do they?' she replied.

Then, he was gone like a pigeon might fly from a window ledge, leaving Sasha wanting one more conversation. 'If you disappear, I may never see you again,' she called out to his departing back.

For a time, everyone around her became her father. She even crossed a street because a man she saw resembled him, until father and daughter were slowly lost to each other piece by piece.

Then one day when she was standing in her pyjamas on her patio, they rang her with the news that Darius had passed away in his sleep, just as his plans for a new life were coming to fruition.

Sasha was astonished, at first, but then felt every painful moment of her father's passing. She was sad she could not be with him when he died and soon came to understand that she would always mourn his death, together with the death of her mother and the death of something in herself.

Now, people know very little about Sasha, and if she is different from others, she likes it that way. She is alone but tells herself she likes living alone. While she has no interest in her father's car and never drives it, she continues to weave what she remembers of him into her singing.

In the silence of the night, she dreams of fame and of being less different. She dreams of being known. There are times when she longs to see Darius's face, his grey hair, grey eyes and grey bathrobe, but there are other times when the colour grey makes her want to cry.

It is nearly midnight. Sasha has been so busy painting her kitchen walls pink that, for her, time has ceased to exist. Elsewhere in London, Claire is with Peter while Sonya, Claire's half-sister, is planning the apple orchard she hopes to plant with her gardener, Jack. Herbert, father to Claire and Sonya, is baking meringues, Lily is buying milk from her corner shop, and Jonas is staring at the stars.

Sasha, who loves pink mainly because it isn't grey, is trying to decide whether the day has passed quickly or slowly. Either way, she is creating her own world, a world for which she is responsible, and has resigned herself to a late night.

Here she is, listening to Mozart's Requiem and wearing a paint spattered shirt over a dress onto which she has sewn heart-shaped buttons. Mozart felt as she feels, she thinks.

She watches the shadows passing cars throw on to her drying walls. She is so proud to see a sparkling result emerge from a simple day that when she opens her front door to air the room, she calls out 'Hello' because you never know. She peers into the darkened hallway. Nothing. Then Lily, who is returning, passes by.

'Lovely warm night for April,' Lily says.

All you need in the world is one friend, thinks Sasha. She steps out of her door and says, 'My walls make the warm night seem even warmer, you know.'

Lily doesn't know but nods her head.

'Would you like to see my walls?' Sasha's face shines with hope.

'Not now – but thank you,' says Lily.

They say goodnight and Sasha hears the soft closing of a door before she returns to her kitchen where the light from a lamp turns everything into a hazy mingling of pink and yellow. She blows dust off shiny surfaces and plans to pin photographs of birds all around because birds haven't a care in the world. Job done. Then she packs away her paints and looks out at the moon hanging in a sky which seems far away and starless. Next, she tugs her lace curtains together and, because there is nowhere for her to go except to sleep, she switches off the lights.

She prays by the side of her bed as she does every night and every morning, and falls asleep under her flowery quilt, imagining the presence of a lover lying beside her, calling her Alice and asking her to sing. Then the moon caresses her home as if blessing a day well spent while her walls, quiet as they are, seem to thrum with their own stories.

In the world outside, spring murmurs, a dog barks and owls hoot – sounds rarely heard in London, while subway trains rumble and hiss their way along tracks and the sky is painted purple upon purple into deeper shades of night.

PURPLE

Jonas sinks to his knees and stares at the moon. He loves staring at the moon. By its light, he peers at the label of his shapeless coat and is about to put it on and return to his room because it's after midnight, because a sense of unease has come over him, and because it is better to face things than to run away. But the velvet night, smelling of hyacinths and newly mown grass, descends like a warm blanket, so low he feels he can touch it.

Coming to the park was a good idea. His spirits lift. The night is his friend. He can't see the duck pond, but he can hear it breathe. He pushes his coat and notebook under the bench and lets Lily float through his mind till sleep takes her away. The last sounds he hears are the hum of a car cruising the neighbourhood, and the buzz of a cicada brought, by chance, into the city from the New Forest. Then he settles his back against the bench and drapes his arms over his head like a turban. Silence descends.

Good night. Good night.

But he is restless. His mind remains full of questions to which there are no answers. Some questions are best left unanswered.

He opens his eyes again and sees a loitering fox. A night can seem endless. Morning may never come.

Then he imagines he is still awake when he is already asleep and he remains on his bench till the sun begins its rise over London, Sunday becomes Monday, and the first birds sing.

PINK

Sasha wakes as the first birds serenade. It is her thirty-ninth birthday, and she is glad to catch the early sun's rays because she missed the stars. Dawn is when she feels herself most keenly; it's a time of promise when night and day mingle. She takes her tea and buttered toast with honey to her patio to whisper encouragement to her plants and watch the birds dip their wings into the birdbath.

Birds bring her secrets from another world, she thinks, and she spends nearly an hour throwing seeds into the air while birds pose on plants to catch them.

As Sasha stands there this Monday morning, wearing her pyjamas and her late mother's shawl, she rejoices in the way the birds take her seeds and thinks how funny and how simple life is.

She checks her watch. It is ten to seven. She is happy to stand where she is, watching the sunrise colour the sky. This is her little piece of London and, as far as she is concerned, it could be a quiet town at the edge of the world where the clouds look like feathers dropped from a giant flamingo on to the dawn.

PURPLE

Jonas opens his eyes. Daylight has come around and it is quarter past seven. Minutes have turned into hours, and hours into a new day. He isn't sure, at first, what day it is. It could be Sunday, or it could be Monday; all early mornings are alike in spring. He doesn't own a watch and trying to make sense of time is like trying to make sense of music or changing seasons, but he does think that time passes differently for different people.

The grass is wet with dew, trees are loud with birds, there are no stars left in the sky and the clouds are too high to resemble anything. Jonas feels that God has woken him early so that he can witness the sun rise on this beautiful scene. There is a reason why morning follows night, he thinks. Still, he is the only person in the park, and doesn't want to face the day. He was having a better time asleep. Ahead of him is another empty morning.

He picks up a frog which seems to be hopping with difficulty along a path and carries it carefully to the grass, where he spends a while staring at it under the sun's gently swelling light. When he finally steps into the day, he does so with steps so tentative, he appears to be stepping backwards. He leaves the park with plans to return to his room, weigh up his options and count his savings such as they are, because he often thinks about money even though he has next to none.

He begins his walk under a pale sky, past houses which are still unlit and houses where parents and children can be seen through the windows; all these lives, he thinks, all these stories he'll never know. He amuses himself by imagining how he might live in such houses if only he had the money.

While Jonas isn't sure whether he is happy or not right now, there are people in London who are. Herbert is baking his best meringues ever, Sasha is delighting in her walls' pinkness, Peter feels lucky to have spent a night with Claire and Sonya is standing in her garden full of spring's shoots, feeling wonder at the new season's growth.

April is a month when seasons blend into one another, and Jonas can't know that winter's final push is about to bring more snow to the city than has fallen since December. Spring stirs up feelings, but its pink blossom, blushing dog roses and light skies don't interest Jonas, nor is snow his concern.

BLUE

When Claire wakes, she wonders how a flat in the centre of a city can be as quiet as hers feels. Her bedside clock says seven thirty-five. She fears the passage of time which will only seem relentless if she keeps checking its progress. Peter has left, and it troubles her that she can't decide whether he is good-looking or not.

She looks out at the square from behind a chintz curtain; there are few signs of life apart from hovering gulls which drop to the statue of Charles James Fox, bickering for scraps. Lights are on in some apartments and through an open window come sounds of a clarinettist practising for a recital which will be broadcast later this afternoon.

Claire opens all the windows and throws Peter's chocolates into a bin. Her napkins go into the laundry basket. She smooths the sheets on her bed, still rumpled from lovemaking. By way of habit, she peeps into her home office which doubles as a guest bedroom; at the rows of jackets and skirts hanging in the cupboard, the glow of a computer screen and the toothbrushes standing at the ready before softly closing the door. She plumps the cushions then rings Herbert, her once absent father whom she doesn't understand. There is no end to the questions she would like to ask, so she phones him every Monday. She doesn't ask her questions because awkwardness gets in her way. She would like to ask him about her half- sister, Sonya. She would like to say, 'I spent years wondering about you and Sonya with a confused kind of longing. Now, I see myself as the daughter of a man who married twice – that's all.' But she never does.

She peels and slices an apple, her favourite fruit, and brews tea, which she drinks weak and black with a slice of lemon from a porcelain cup before making three unsuccessful attempts to ring Lily. She is obliged to say, 'Hello. Hello? You aren't answering. Are you asleep?' into the answering machine. Her voice sounds small, and she leaves an audible sip of tea.

Then she sits in her favourite chair and waits. This time, she doesn't know for whom or what she is waiting, except that all her waiting feels like it is pushing against her. She has laughed, cried and told Peter more than once that she never wants to see him again from this chair. But now, she lets her thoughts settle on her flat and on the fact that a great deal of her care has gone into it and that it has a soul which loves her no matter what. And this is just as well because last night's visitors left her feeling like a stranger in her own home. Then her thoughts return to Lily because this is where they want to be; she would have a place in the world if Lily needed her, she reflects.

And while she is thinking this, the passion she found the night before dances on the curtains and walls, knocking the room's colour-coded orderliness a little off kilter.

WHITE

Herbert was a lieutenant colonel in the British army during the
Second World War and, while he may not look it, he celebrated
his 89th birthday a week ago when the stars formed in the shape
of the ram's horns of the Aries sign – or so his daughter Claire
explained.

He is tall and bony with large hands, and age has made him
no less handsome; his face remains open and kind even if he has
whiskery white eyebrows and must wear glasses without which he
would appear slightly vulnerable. Where once he climbed steps,
taking two at a time, he now walks with a limp after a knee
replacement – and with the aid of a stick. But he still squats as
best he can especially when talking to Lily, his grandchild.

Herbert is a dreamer who isn't going to let a mere limp stand
in his way. If frailty forces him to give up on one dream, he will
try another. He married twice to women both named Annette,
but they are now dead, and he lives alone. Still, solitude doesn't
prevent his dreaming as often as he chooses, and he doesn't have
to share his dreams. He can sit in his house thinking thoughts no-
one else needs understand, and with no wife to suggest he rise
from his chair and do something else. And if a passing stranger
asks why he appears to be talking to himself, he can reply that he
is simply having a conversation with the past and he is at peace
with that.

And peace for Herbert means spending as much time as
possible on his own. His focus is on staying alive in this house,

which is as still as the houses around it, each of them filled now with soft morning light and the quiet of people known to him only by sight, who are probably thinking as he is, about the past.

GREEN

Far away in Hampstead, a leafy north London parkland where trees grow in every shade of green and where there are meadows for summer concerts and a lido where brave people swim in winter, Sonya, Herbert's daughter from his second marriage, and Claire's half-sister, opens her eyes on the day.

It troubles Sonya that she has not kept her once slender figure and that her short curly hair is turning grey. However, people say her eyes light up like leaves in sunshine. Back in the day, she wanted to be a professional tennis player and she played for her club, but things didn't work out as planned.

Sonya would prefer to live in the countryside, but, on a day like today when her house smells like flowers after April showers, she decides that she mustn't complain. She has a pond in her garden where sticklebacks swim and if anyone asks why she lives where she does, she replies, 'For the moment, we like it here.'

Sonya's house would be wonderful for parties if she gave parties; on good days, it is sunny in summer and warm in winter and the front door with its brass handle lets colour in from the garden every time Sonya opens it. When she bought her house, the garden was nothing to speak of, but it is so beautiful now that people sometimes pause to admire it. The walls on the inside of the house are painted cream, there are wooden floors, and the long, narrow windows are bare, all the better to see the shadows cast by the surrounding trees.

Ever since Sonya was a child, her half-sister Claire lived in the shadows in Sonya's mind. Sonya often thinks how sad it is that Claire's mother never forgave Herbert for leaving for her mother, the other Annette, and it's odd to think that Sonya barely knows Lily. She and Claire don't speak. But still.

WHITE

It is nearly eight o'clock. Herbert is dressed now in linen jacket and trousers with his Fedora on his head, and is seated in his small garden, enjoying the fragrances of jasmine and dog rose.

Time is moving on, he muses, as he watches the dawn pull back the last of the night. What joy! He never had time to stare at the dawn when he worked as a teacher.

'You wake on some days, and everything is perfect,' he says smiling to himself - and he knows the day will be perfect because he listened to the weather forecast; weather is important.

He closes his eyes and feels the early morning sun glow yellow on his eyelids. Waves of gratitude sweep through him. He is grateful for the taste of his biscuits and cakes and for the sound of choral music. He is grateful to sit where he is and to be able to sit unnoticed. Yes, he thinks, solitude, once so painfully felt, is now freeing and comes with the blessings of peace and space. He is far from ready to leave this world.

Herbert once inspired Lily and hundreds of others with his love of learning. These days, he spends a good deal of his time baking and uses only butter cream not fondant on his cakes. When he is happy, he bakes. When there is trouble, he bakes. He bakes cakes on Fridays to sell in a market on Saturdays and whistles tunes while baking, whatever is in his mixing bowl.

'The measuring and mixing soothe me,' he tells his cleaner, who visits once a week and thinks she knows everything about him. 'When I bake, everything is fine. And when my patience with baking fades, the notion that I once laughed the loudest, loved the deepest and baked the best coffee-walnut cakes in the market, will be a comfort.'

'Yes,' says his cleaner, 'Yes. Do you ever wish you were young again?' and she stands on tiptoes and shouts because he is so tall.

While she sees his baking only in terms of the cinnamon and icing sugar he scatters, she is proud that his curtains are white and starched. They have been together for so long that when they talk, they talk as if they were both still young.

'Never,' is his reply, 'I'm grateful that things unfold as they must. I'm thankful for days which roll out at their own pace. I'm thankful for this ordinary life.'

His cleaner, who loves his courtly manners and thinks he has the most expressive face she has seen, is constantly amazed at the wisdom he imparts.

'He is a shining example of how to live on earth,' she tells her husband, 'And he has such a pretty house.'

But these days, Herbert lives more in his mind than on earth. He might be saying something when a wave of memory comes along and washes over him with such force, he is obliged to sit. If there are times when he can't shake off the gentle sadness which the years have placed on his shoulders, there are others when he casts his mind back to his proudest moment, his escape from the beaches of Dunkirk. Herbert often thinks of the time when he stood on a beach in darkness – the kind which blots out all hope – waiting for dawn to break and not expecting to live past sunrise until he was rescued by a British destroyer and taken to Dover and safety. To this day he still wears the wristwatch he wore in Dunkirk as a reminder that there was a moment when all he could do was keep going, and when staying alive was the most difficult choice of all.

Not a day passes when Herbert doesn't think of his daughters, Claire and Sonya, and his wives, the two Annettes whose stories flow like a river through everything which is meaningful to him. He raises his mug of tea with two sugars and toasts their stories.

'If I have made mistakes, if I left one Annette for another, and if there are tiny lines of sorrow on my face, they will dissolve into lines of happiness when the steam rises from my tea. All things considered, I am happy as I can be,' he tells a little sparrow even if he knows full well that there are situations which mere happiness can't handle. So be it.

BROWN

Peter left Claire at sunrise. He left a note; 'I love you and miss you already' after crossing out then re-inserting 'miss you already.' Stupid, he thought. Next, he signed the note with kisses, gathered his jacket from the dining table, and took the lift to the street, where the air was still cool from the night. Once seated in his car, he waited for nearly two hours, smoking and thinking about Claire and about his future, while listening to Ella Fitzgerald sing 'My Happiness' on the radio. 'Where I am right now might be in the middle of one of the happiest years of my life so far,' he told Ella Fitzgerald.

Now, it is eight-thirty. Time waits for no man. He decides to stop for a coffee before returning home and drives away just as two seagulls swoop past, dangerously close to his windscreen and miles from the sea. He thinks about time flying and about Monday. He needs to get going; get to work. Claire's hands distract him again by visiting him out of the blue, but he pulls himself together. 'Claire may be Claire,' he says out loud. 'She saves me and that's the truth, but work is work.'

He walks into a café and positions himself at the bar, deciding to stay close to Claire in the future because his life depends on it. Yes, it is what it is, he reflects.

PINK

Just to be sure, Sasha checks the time. It is nearly nine. She showers and dresses with care, tucks her hair into a scarf and sticks heart earrings in her earlobes. Then she buys hyacinths at a flower stall and makes her way to the cemetery; a solitary woman visiting her mother's grave on this, the day of her thirty-ninth birthday.

When Sasha arrives at the cemetery, the only signs of life are a pale green butterfly, a seagull and her bunch of hyacinths, of course, but the sun is shining, and the weather is warm and promising.

She tries to pray and whispers 'thank you for being my mother and for taking care of me throughout your life and even in death' but she doesn't stay long. She simply pays her respects then sets off for the café where she works as a waitress when there are no auditions for her to attend or requests for her to sing. She is popular among staff and clients in the café and there is always someone on a bar stool trying to make eye contact with her because she can see many sides of situations and she knows how to listen. But no-one guesses that while she has no wish to talk about herself, she hopes that someone will ask her name so she can reply 'Alice'.

Sasha arrives late but, once there, hands Peter, a regular customer and an ordinary man who has been waiting as if he expected someone, a two shot Americano.

'There you go,' she says, serving him with grace he will remember even if her mind is not focused on him.

'Thank you,' he says.

'You're welcome,' she says.

Peter puts sugar in his cup then absently begins a conversation but not before looking through his bifocals at the traces of paint on her hands. At least her fingernails are clean, he thinks. He says, 'There is nothing better than a decent cup of coffee. I don't know if I've told you, but my name is Peter – P-E-T-E-R.'

She knows his name and is used to his ways so she doesn't reply but, instead, secretly admires his tie and matching waistcoat and wishes she could say, 'call me Alice.'

'Tell me about yourself,' he tries again, 'Were you born in London – although being a Londoner has nothing to do with where you were born? Do you know what I mean?' he asks.

She doesn't, but she nods and smiles.

'Me?' she replies, 'do you need anything else?'

She decides not to tell him that this is her thirty-ninth birthday and that her late father said that her birthday coincides with the day in spring when blossoms are at their most scented.

He shakes his head and tastes his coffee; black and sweet, exactly what he wants. His hands tremble as the taste of the coffee mingles with the taste of his difficulty in making a living, which is never far from the back of his throat.

He is scared, he thinks, because he doesn't know where to go from here. On the other hand, he could well be one cup of coffee away from solving everything – life being life.

She watches him drink. 'Is it alright?' she asks, giving him a hopeful thumbs up. People tell her things. She doesn't know why.

He studies her face. Something about her makes him want to share his life story and to explain that he is childless and a widower, but he stops short because he suspects she might be in the middle of her own life story and because he fears she might say, 'let me tell you about MY life.'

'Life is life,' he says, 'life is not easy, but life is not difficult. Life has a way of working out.' He likes this line and warms to it as he speaks.

'Do you really think so?' she asks, 'I'm thinking of leaving my life in this city for a while.'

'How much do I owe you?' he evades her question.

Pain moves across her face. She mistakes his indifference for disapproval.

A week ago, Peter asked if she had a boyfriend and she lied and said, 'oh he died', because she finds it easier to lie than explain that she knows what it's like to wait in a cafe for a man who never shows up.

Peter stares out of the window.

He thinks about Claire again and surprises himself by thinking about Lily. What is she like? Should he ask Sasha whether she has children? He lives his life with the shadow of not having any.

'What are you thinking?' Sasha asks, touching her heart earrings which twinkle like tiny prisms of light and staring at him for what feels like a moment too long. Because she likes the sound of his voice, she wants Peter to keep talking.

'Nothing. It doesn't matter,' he replies, and his left eye begins to twitch because the fleeting sense of recognition which has passed between them – albeit there and then gone – troubles him. He looks at her then looks away. He is not one to put people down, he thinks, and life has taught him to respect others' needs but he has no further need for conversation. He has a life.

She is about to continue talking but realises the atmosphere between them has changed. If she is hurt, she hides it well. She curls her fingers around her coffee cup, smiling bravely through her disappointment. Then she helps herself to a carrot cupcake with cream cheese icing because it's her birthday. She sips her coffee while glancing at Peter. She is happy enough with the spring sunlight she can see through the windows and the ordinary faces she sees all around give some respite from her solitude. But she is still having the kind of day when she realises that life might be moving forward without her the way life can, and when she fears that she might be one of those women people pass in the street without seeing. If anyone were to ask how her life is now, she would not know what to say.

Peter decides to leave the cafe. There are many moments of kindness in this city, and this may well be one, but he needs to go home.

'I must return to my birds,' says Sasha as if reading his thoughts. Then she wipes the counter between them before taking a broom to the floor.

Her shift is ending, and she does have birds to feed, but she dreads her solitary walk home, and a solitary birthday walk, at that.

'You're a nice person,' Peter says, putting money on the counter between them and kissing her cheeks – one kiss on each. 'Enjoy your day.' Then they part like two ordinary people who have spent a tired hour together.

Sasha leaves the café and starts walking, initially looking like someone who isn't sure where she is going and feeling like someone who has somehow failed a secret test. But the sun is shining so brightly for the time of year, that this feeling is soon forgotten, and she gives thanks for the beauty of the sky as if it were a sky in a story, painted with strawberries and belonging to everyone. She begins to feel happier. If asked, she would have to say she feels happy because of the sky's pinkness.

She changes her step to that of an urban person, someone she imagines to be detached and solitary, but interesting; an urban person who knows about other peoples' routines, their habits and their clothes, but absolutely nothing else. In the same way, she knows that there are untold stories behind the faces of people who drink alone in cafes and that there are private lives unfolding behind every door in the city – as they must.

BROWN

Fortified by coffee, Peter drives home lost in thoughts which have nothing to do with anyone else.

He looks in the rear-view mirror. His face is square, and his silver hair is slicked back at the sides. Although he is fifty-three, he feels older and a little broken. He is afraid of ageing, his voice is husky from years of smoking, and he has bulked out although he used to be thin. On a good day he likes to think that he looks like a young Kirk Douglas, whom he once regarded as a secret friend.

Peter's wife died shortly after they married, leaving him with a profound sense of personal failure, although he knows that there was nothing at all he could do to prevent it. There are days when he misses her, and other days when he thinks of her simply as one might think of sunshine. Now he lives alone and manages – more or less. Not the way he did when she was alive, of course, but still. They lived in a house in Southgate which had roses he pruned in the front garden and clematis he pruned in the back. It never occurred to Peter that his wife wouldn't last the course. When he drives past the house in Southgate – albeit rarely – he averts his eyes.

He enjoys driving and he enjoys speed. Nowadays, it is his car which is his most constant companion; he is emotional about cars, and he loves wheels, even steering wheels. Because he smokes, he keeps mints in the glove compartment of his car, and he often drives around after dark, cigarette between his fingers, mint in his mouth and with no destination in mind. His father was a car mechanic, and his clearest childhood memory is of working beside him in the garage during his school holidays. When his father lay dying on the garage floor, Peter sat beside him, holding his hand. His father said, 'Remember, son, it's not the car you drive, but how you drive it. It doesn't matter how big your car is, it only matters how much your heart can hold.'

Even so, if you hurt Peter's car, you hurt his heart.

Peter's thoughts turn to Kirk Douglas. Had he been lucky enough to meet Kirk, he would have asked him if he liked cars. He would have asked about Hollywood. But what sort of man would trouble another this way?

'I am not a man to trouble another,' he says out loud, but he does marvel at how happy the film star was to do things his way and at the fact that he was married to the same woman for more than sixty years. When Kirk died, Peter cried.

Now, he is driving slowly, with one arm draped out of the window and devoting his journey to keeping awake. He is trying not to crash his car because, although the morning is clear and bright like a morning in summer, it is spring and there is spring dust in his eyes. He is also experiencing a familiar aching pressure in his chest and not for the first time, especially when he feels too warm. It passes – thankfully – but the warmth in the car is intense and made worse by the fact that he is wearing a waistcoat under his jacket and a tie – all slightly behind the fashion curve, he acknowledges, but never mind.

He drives as carefully as he can through Paddington Basin, passing small brown houses then large white houses, and with the busyness of the city around him. He loves the sounds and smells of traffic and opens all the windows, despite the air conditioning being on high, and the breeze blowing more dust and the combined scents of car exhaust fumes and trees into his face.

He stops at lights. While he is listening to warnings of traffic delays on his radio, music blasts from a neighbouring car. The rhythm of the music catches Peter, making him feel like a dancer trapped in a cage. Why do some people imagine that everyone else likes the music they do? It doesn't matter. People are born and people die, seasons change, rivers flow to the sea and we are all lucky enough to be a part of it for a while, he reflects.

For now, it's a simple matter of waiting for the red light to turn green.

He is aware of the pressure of his foot on the pedal. He taps an impatient finger on the steering wheel and studies his hands which are leathery, dotted with black hair and unusually large for his size. You can tell a great deal from hands, he thinks; how they wait, snatch, hesitate. You can see a calculating man in a steady hand, a desperate one in a shaking hand, an anxious one in a clasped hand. He thinks about the hands which have shaped him, hands which have caressed him, hands which paid him, hands which led him to trouble and his mother's large, lined, calloused hands.

When the light goes green, his mother's hands slip out of memory's view and he turns again to look at the shapes London is making through the windows. London is always winding down then beginning anew. Everything stays the same, yet nothing stays the same. Where did those brown buildings spring from? He has spent more time driving through central London than living in it. He thinks about London; he loves London like he would a person. London can be uncomfortable and inconvenient, he thinks, but he loves the noise and the dirt, the mismatched architecture, terraced houses, tube lines, clubs, pubs, places of worship, charity shops, millions of trees and pigeons which roost on monuments.

He edges forward but an urban fox with a sly smile, out and about further and later than usual, swaggers across the road in front of him on its way back to its den. The fox is in no hurry. Peter studies it until it disappears in a sunny haze, and he wishes he could live like a fox, leaving people to resolve things themselves without his having to think about them.

The light turns back to red, and a taxi driver honks his horn. London life. Nothing special, thinks Peter, but, nonetheless, London traffic never used to be like this.

At last, he can move, and soon he eases his car as carefully as possible into a parking space near the house where he now lives, thinking that however fine London looks from a driving seat, no city is real till you get out of your car. His journey has taken so long that he has broken the promise he made to visit his sister.

He sits in his car for a while, twisting his worry beads around and around his fingers and thinking about Claire and about his late wife and wondering at his taste in women and whether he knows anything about women at all or about himself.

He loved his late wife. There are mornings when he has such a clear image of her sitting in their house in Southgate, where he painted the walls and sanded the floors, that he longs to be taken back to that 1930s building and almost cries out her name. His late wife has been on his mind a lot recently in a way which has nothing to do with his love for Claire. What kind of man would he be if his thoughts left her simply because she is dead, he reflects. He reminds himself that the house in Southgate is no longer his and tries, instead, to imagine what sort of people the new owners are. We may leave a place. This doesn't mean the place leaves us. But even if a house follows you like a shadow, he thinks, you always lose something when you move house.

His present home seems smaller, somehow, than he remembered. When he enters it, his tinted bifocals are still on his nose and he waits for them to adjust before he can say, 'I am here' to the hollow sounding rooms and largely bare walls. His plan was to decorate then move on and there are cushions scattered around and a few houseplants, but after a year, he hasn't done much.

He goes into his home office, takes off his jacket and sits at his desk, looking at the wall opposite. He is self-employed and invests in a small way in this and that, but never knows where his next pay is coming from and doesn't have anything like enough to do. In fact, he has less money than anyone realises. Still, business is business, however small. It must be. He removes his bifocals and wipes them with the hem of his shirt. He pours himself a whisky. His hand is shaking. He takes his time.

'I drink too much,' he says out loud.

He rings his sister.

'Dear God, Peter, you forgot,' she says, 'It was today, wasn't it? I can't believe you forgot – except I can. Why do I care?'

He makes a noise of weariness. Winds his worry beads around his fingers. 'I don't know. I'm not myself. I was with Claire. You get into things. You don't pay attention. You don't realise what you're getting into – there's always something to worry about. Do you ever feel that way?' he tries to explain but is too tired.

'Who is Claire?' asks his sister.

'Just a person I know,' he replies before disconnecting, but with a moment of regret because family is family.

He continues to stare at the flaking windowsills and at the wall and the endless depths of brown. After a while, he stops seeing brown and sees Claire's refined hands and her face instead, so cold and yet so pretty, and this image is so real it startles him especially as he can't reconcile it with his certain belief that Claire is in her flat in Bloomsbury.

My entire life faces the wall except when I am with Claire, he thinks.

'Claire, I think about you all the time,' he says audibly.

He loosens his tie, takes off his waistcoat and throws away his cigarette packet; he's down to three a day, he thinks with some pride. Then he goes to the fridge and eats what's left of a carton of stir-fry chicken and glass noodles before taking spoonsful of chocolate ice-cream straight from the tub.

He replays his night with Claire but needs to work; work is work. He must keep going. He must keep going because he doesn't know what else to do.

WHITE

If most of his life swells behind him, if old age has crept up unexpectedly, and if time now takes on a different cast, Herbert still studies the wristwatch he wore in Dunkirk. Now, it says eleven thirty-six. He has left Chelsea's green-leafed streets, white terraced houses and spring smells, and is walking with his stick down the King's Road. He passes three cafes, a pharmacy, and a supermarket before checking his appearance in the window of a charity shop. Although he chooses to talk as little as possible these days, he stops and greets people he passes along the way. They greet him back because of his smile, some ask about his past, then talk about theirs. 'How is everything?' some ask. 'Everything is fine,' he replies. Herbert takes his time. The prospect of seeing Lily makes him happy and he walks as if he were walking centimetres off the ground.

'Do you want to dance?' he asks a gull, as he touches the rim of his Fedora.

Then he makes his way to the river, crossing Albert Bridge and entering Battersea Park in sunshine, but with an umbrella hooked over his arm because showers were forecast and because he pays attention to weather forecasts.

He reaches the park earlier than expected so decides to rest on a bench while waiting for Lily. When she arrives, he plans to hand her the meringue shell he baked and filled with lemon cream because it is delicious and because giving matters.

'It really matters,' says Herbert to the morning sky just in case someone up there is listening.

YELLOW

Lily woke with the sun and ran through Battersea Park, passing the bench where Jonas sits, in order to make herself feel that she was doing something. The last signs of winter had disappeared three weeks ago, and spring spread itself over the city, leaving the morning with lilac, cherry blossom and birdsong and with people on buses and trains smiling at one another or saying, 'what a lovely day.'

Now, at ten minutes before midday, those with a feel for weather know that rain is imminent, but the sun could not be shining more brightly, like a golden ball suspended over this roughly circular city, telling everyone to be happy. Those who follow such things, say either that they are happy or that they are not.

Lily is sitting at her dressing table, caught in a sunbeam, and studying her reflection while getting ready to face the day. An old chestnut tree she climbed as a girl leans against the window of the bedroom, and all is tranquil with a stillness which seems to hang down the curtains and nestle into the sofas. Lily wonders if by returning to this sand-coloured house which stood intact for nearly two centuries till it was sub-divided into flats, she has turned into a twenty-four-year-old child. Whatever the case, she feels happy and at ease in sunlight and is glad Sunday has passed into Monday, second day of the week, but with a promise of fresh starts.

There are daisies on the bedroom wallpaper, a braided rug sits on the floor and the paint is peeling off a cream-coloured chest of drawers. On the dressing table is a cloth which is frayed around the edges and a chipped jug of daffodils stands next to the photographs displayed there, one of which was taken on Lily's eleventh birthday, thirteen years ago. In it, she is petite and freckled and – even then – wearing a yellow cardigan draped over a white blouse. Her eyes are innocent, and she is seated and smiling and holding a book while looking straight to camera, unaware that her mother would be gone before the month was out. Although her time spent with Marcus in Cyprus marked the start of her journey from childhood to adulthood, and although it felt good to live in a place where the sun came out and stayed out, Lily has come to think of him as part of a chapter which is closed, and the years spent in Cyprus as left behind like seasons which have passed.

'You have your life. You must live it,' Marcus said when he waved her goodbye, 'you decided to leave, so leave quickly. Never turn back and never believe that anything you experienced here is better than what you are about to experience. People rarely know what they want.'

From that moment on she stopped expecting him to save her, and his remarks made her as angry as the day she watched Claire's suitcases being carried away and her back disappearing through the door. When she asked Marcus at the time where Claire was going, he said, 'We've already discussed this,' but she has no memory of the discussion.

This doesn't mean he didn't say, 'Lily, you are all I have,' or ask Claire, 'Why now?'

Lily opens her bedroom window and in comes life; an aeroplane crosses the window bars; a church spire glints in the sunshine and the breeze sends a small green butterfly on to her carpet. When she helps the butterfly back into the air, she sees a policeman on the pavement below, knocking on the front door of her building and asking for Sasha. The sound of his knocking jumps along the street.

'Which flat are you?' he asks the cluster of doorbells studded on the wall.

Lily looks across the sky towards the church spire.

'I won't be long,' she says to two seagulls winding their way through the air, flapping their wings in unison on their way to the river, and she realises that she is speaking in her mother's voice, trying to sound confident when she is not. 'Why should you have to listen to me?' she asks the birds. Then she drapes a cardigan over her shoulders, checks her hair, runs her hands over the front of her dress, and with a smudge of lipstick and a spritz of perfume, she is ready to face the day.

She is out of her door at midday, and although she often pauses when she leaves her flat, something about this day propels her forward. She puts on sunglasses, runs down the three flights of stairs to the street and steps into the daylight as the warmth of the pavement comes up to greet her. But to be on the safe side, she returns to her flat for her raincoat. Then she closes her door again, leaving the metal hanger where her coat hung swinging in the cupboard.

Lily has arranged to meet Herbert. She makes her way to Battersea Park with its spring smells, green spaces and bright flowers, as if it were the only place on earth, and Herbert, the only person in it.

GREEN

Out of the blue, Sonya's house becomes dark then rain starts beating on the roof, off her trees and against the large windowpanes in the living room. Sonya rushes around, closing windows and switching on lights, then she stands in her bedroom watching the flowers in her garden bend under the weight of water and her fishpond turn slightly choppy.

PINK

Rain falls indiscriminately, as it must, on to the loved and the unloved alike. Drivers put on their wipers and most people run, duck or seek shelter. Sasha, who is caught without a jacket or coat, lets raindrops run down her unprotected face because she loves the rain and because falling rain feels like music with life-enhancing lyrics to her, bringing with it the reminder that she is not alone. When she reaches her home, the sight of water on the leaves of the chestnut tree outside it, warms her heart.

Once inside her flat, the first thing she does after removing her wet clothes and casting a glance at her newly painted walls, is to throw the last of Darius's possessions into the bin.

BLUE

Claire had been meaning to see an exhibition, but the day turned into a shopping day; shopping is her refuge. Now, fortified by tea and scones and the prospect of opening and sorting her parcels, she steps into a puddle before climbing into a taxi. 'Bloomsbury Square,' she says, looking at her sodden shoes, 'and fast, please.' The thought crosses her mind that she changes men like shoes because she fears they won't find enough reasons to stay. The driver hasn't driven long before she wonders if he is laughing at her. She needs to return to the familiarity of her home, she thinks. All will be well when she closes her door on the rain.

PURPLE

Jonas continues his slow way home despite the rain. This is one of the times when he acts as if he's the only person in this city. He imagines Lily by his side and splashes softly through puddles for fear of disturbing the ghosts of people who have walked the same streets before him. He is one such person. No more. No less.

When he enters his room, it is eleven minutes past twelve. While time passes differently for him, this morning is moving on like any other. He closes his door. It is grey outside and in the dim inside light the details of the photograph on his wall can't be seen from certain angles. The cyclist in it seems to have disappeared and all Jonas can make out is the tree. He pushes away the fanciful thought that the cyclist may have needed saving; it is his mind playing cruel tricks, of course.

And all the while his notebook with its yellowing pages together with his coat are sheltering under the park bench, both as shapeless now as any objects the rain finds in its way.

YELLOW

It is quarter past twelve. Falling rain melts all the colours of the world together, thinks Lily. She puts on her raincoat and is about to cross a street when a teenage boy driving a stolen car she recognises as Sasha's, slams a cyclist into the back of Peter's parked Volvo before speeding away from the scene. Nobody knows why.

The cyclist's name is Jack, he is twenty-seven, unmarried and works as a gardener. Yesterday Jack was alive, today he is dying. Fate has intervened and an accident occurs. Shoots inside Jack snap, his future is taken from him, and he will never plant the apple trees he and Sonya planned to grow in her garden.

Nothing prepared Lily for this.

The same two seagulls which fluttered from rooftop to rooftop on their way to the river drop to the pavement as if in shock and as if to distract Lily, who averts her gaze from the injured cyclist and his mangled bicycle to the rain filled sky. Then she looks again in confusion at the gulls and at the broken, odd-shaped strands of glass scattered in puddles which make her feel as if small pieces of her own life lie strewn among the glass. Her first impulse is to run forward and do something – anything – and if this is the moment when her life changes for ever, she doesn't notice because everything is happening too fast.

Traffic accidents make people appear out of nowhere. Hands reach out. Words pour down like rain. People say, 'I am sorry. I am sorry.' Someone says, 'There is no sound in the world like a car crash.' Someone says, 'Accidents like this take place every day.' Someone says, 'Most drivers should have their licences temporarily suspended.' Someone says, 'This has nothing to do with me.' Someone says, 'My day began like any other...' Someone asks if the cyclist is breathing and adds, 'Both his legs are crushed.' Some will remember the scene like a photograph, and some move out of the way. And all the while the sky weeps while Jack lies still as a stone.

An ambulance approaches. Lily sees a life's ending dance before her and, while this is the end for someone marginal, it feels so central to her at this moment, that she understands her own death. She thinks about the cyclist's parents, who might be on their way to work or walking the dog, not knowing that their son is dying, and she understands that if she were to die, Claire would miss her.

Her eyes well and she can't see anything aside from her tears. She can't breathe and she shakes all over.

'How quickly everything changes,' someone says as the rain stops, and the realisation settles that a man is dying – a man who was alive just hours ago and a man like any other, whose passing will soon become as unremarkable as rain.

The account of the accident tears along the street and will tear through London, seeping into relationships and deeply held convictions and changing lives. For some, it provides the opportunity to unleash emotions long held in check, while others speak about it in supermarkets, over the telephone and outside schools until it becomes one of countless such stories which for most city dwellers, don't matter after a time.

And while this is happening, ordinary people who don't know about the accident go to work or to school or to the cinema; they travel on trains, meet in cafes or put children to sleep. Ordinary people such as Claire, who is thinking about Charles James Fox, or Peter, who is asleep at his desk, or Sasha who is clearing out the last of Darius's possessions, or Jonas, who is staring at the photograph on his bedroom wall, or Sonya who is planning her apple orchard, or Herbert, who is sheltering on a bench under a tree, waiting for Lily.

Back in Lily's flat, the hands of her bedside clock worry their way around from morning to afternoon because people go out and don't return and because everything can change in a single day and because there is nothing as empty as an empty house in spring.

Lily decides to return home now the rain has dissolved into the day's warmth and dark clouds have rolled away to reveal white fluffy ones. The sun surprises her by coming out again and shining over the city. Lily feels like a different person, neither fearful nor sorrowful particularly, but disconnected. Her hair hangs in wet strands over her face, her head spins, and her hands tremble so violently she can barely place her key in the lock.

She rings Claire who does not pick up even though the phone rings and continues to ring. She pictures Claire's room with its white walls and blue upholstered chairs, but she leaves no message. For a while she just sits with her hands on her stomach, rocking back and forth. 'Oh my God. Oh my God,' she says. Then she remembers her arrangement to meet Herbert.

BROWN

Peter's left eye twitches and his legs ache. The effects of the coffee have worn off and he is more exhausted than he realises. If there are tears of tiredness rising inside him, he suppresses them. He folds his arms on his desk, drops his head to them and stumbles into one bad dream after another as London shrinks to a sliver and disappears from his mind and a police car comes to a halt at his front door.

When he hears about his car, Peter asks, 'I don't believe this. WHAT happened to my car?'

A hard blow like lightning strikes his heart.

He rings Claire and leaves a message; 'Where are you? I need you. What's the matter with you?'

For a moment he wishes his late wife were alive and with him – just for a moment. He should have kept his last cigarette.

WHITE

Beneath a sky filled with starlings, Herbert embraces the quiet emptiness which surrounds him while his damp Fedora sits companionably by his side. He scratches his head because raindrops are falling on him from the tree above, then he stares at the duckpond, marvelling at the way the sun lights the water. Lily is late but he can't wait to see her. He plans to let her know how much she resembles her mother and imagines every possible conversation with her, except the one he is about to have. He is also aware that he is an old man, one of many in this city, and that he should be used to being patient. So much of living requires patience, he thinks. He sits for a while, happy not to care about what he is thinking. A pale green butterfly lands on his lap as if to ask, 'Are you expecting someone?' He brushes it off and watches it flap its way towards the clouds. The sun beats down on him, so he takes off his jacket and tie, puts them under the bench together with his walking stick, and bows his head. Soon, he is asleep, and dreaming of the time when he was young and strong and had endurance to match, with eyes which were bright and hearing, sound. He dreams about wading into the sea, dressed in his British army uniform and wearing army boots and holding his rifle above his head as proudly as any other. Anyone looking on might be forgiven for supposing that he is just an old man, either sleeping on a park bench under drying leaves, or that he will never move again.

Time passes. The shadows the trees cast move across the grass. Herbert wakes and checks his watch. Ten to two and still no sign of Lily. He reaches under the bench for his jacket and tie and, to his surprise, finds with them a crumpled coat and a notebook with a faded cover marked 'Jonas's poems.' He opens the notebook and reads. At first, he feels what the poet feels. He, too, has slept in the open, he, too, hasn't known the way home. But then, descriptions of a girl begin to fill the pages; a girl who runs through the park, has yellow hair, a gap between her front teeth and a pale complexion. If this girl isn't Lily, then he doesn't know who is. What is he reading? How can this be? Ten minutes pass. Herbert takes off his glasses and blushes to the roots of his hair. A kind of quiet disbelief goes through him.

'Where is Lily?' he cries, 'I must see her.'

GREEN

More than anything in the world, Sonya hopes that she and Claire will meet again and that there will come a time when their relationship heals. She often plans their reunion in her head, practising her lines and deciding not to say anything which might cause offence because there is no-one whose approval she needs more.

For now, she enjoys moving through her lovely house, rejoicing in the windows, wooden floors and old fireplaces. She feels almost settled here although the house is too big for a woman on her own and, after a year, unpacked boxes containing ornaments and paintings remain dotted about and some of the furniture is still covered with sheets.

Ah well, thinks Sonya, pots and plates are mainly where they should be, clothes are in cupboards and shelves are piled high with books wedged between dog-shaped bookends.

'One day...' she sighs as she hangs a faded sampler embroidered with the words, 'Grow where you are planted' on her bedroom wall. Some of the trees she planted as saplings are so tall now, they are nearly as high as the house. Herbert explained that trees are like people, but wiser because they stand for centuries just watching life go by. Even the tallest trees began life as seeds, he said.

These days, trees give Sonya strength and joy. Without them, she would feel exposed. But there are pockets of sadness amid her joy; she finds some of the women in her neighbourhood intimidating. They guard the details of their lives, and their eyes seem to float above her face when they speak to her. She fears that they see her as a solitary old lady who clings to the past and can't move on; a woman who stands on the fringes of things, making judgements. Wealthy though she may be, there are days when she feels that by comparison to these fragrant women, she smells of new mown grass. This does not prevent her dreaming of a life where they visit in order to admire her flowers and eat beautiful salads and cold cuts in the shade of the sycamores, or pick pears and damsons from her trees.

Sonya never married. She told a man she loved him, but slowly changed her mind. Now, she tells this story to the women in her neighbourhood in the hope that it will turn out differently in the re-telling. 'One day your life is one way, the next, it is not. God knows, I should know,' she says, 'Still, I have forgiven myself. I forgive everyone. We say some things can't be forgiven, but we must forgive all the time.'

All this doesn't prevent her from talking to the man she left, telling him how strange it is that he has remained in her thoughts, explaining that she has changed and hoping he might reply, 'Have you really?'

Now, spring ripples the surface of the fishpond then taps on her windows like a visiting sister, bringing her thoughts back to the present. Time is passing. She has no plans for the day and the afternoon stretches out before her like a quilt. It is twelve minutes past two. Sonya loves cooking as much as Herbert loves baking, and she particularly loves cooking with produce from her garden. She freezes batches of tomato, carrot and marrow soups and sauces, and has jars of damson jam and quince jelly displayed on her kitchen shelves.

She brews coffee and makes French toast. She dips bread carefully into beaten egg, fries it in butter, then covers it with plum jam before slicing and eating it while thinking that most of the joy in her life right now comes from the sweetness of food.

Food and coffee restore her. She holds her cup in both hands, feeling its warmth and taking it to the window where she stands plainly, wrapped in spring sunshine. She needs this drink, she thinks. But soon her thoughts leave the room and are drawn to the garden.

She will never forget the first morning her newly planted garden took shape.

'Look at the Guelder roses. Look at the forsythia,' she said to Jack when shoots began to pop out of once barren soil and seeds sprouted among tulips and grape hyacinths. 'I do love spring and those clouds – I didn't know clouds could be like this, but what do I know?'

She loves her garden whatever the season. She loves how changing months make the garden feel like a character with many different personalities. She loves amber autumns, pearly white winters and blue summers but she particularly loves green springs. It is always spring somewhere in the world, she thinks. A comforting thought.

Now, Monday afternoon's stillness hangs over the garden. If the apple trees which once grew there are now gone – even their stumps are gone – at least three damson and two pear trees remain.

Sonya regards Jack as something of a miracle. He mows her grass, weeds her beds, prunes her roses, feeds the fish in the pond and will replant the apple orchard while spring lasts as spring is the best season for planting apples. 'As you know, our city's variable climate is particularly suited to apple cultivation,' she tells her neighbours with some confidence, then wonders if she sounds a little self-important.

Beyond the fruit trees and roses are magnolia trees which display the first of their flowers. Sonya continues to drink her coffee but soon her eyes blur out of focus, and she no longer takes in the garden but begins, instead, to stare into a magnolia filled landscape in her head. Claire is walking towards her through rows of flowering magnolias, full of appreciation for the garden's beauty.

'Who would have imagined?' asks Claire, 'Everything is happy, thank you Sonya.'

'Ok,' says Sonya. She wants to believe Claire but has learnt to be wary of happiness and has gathered all sorts of evidence that everything is not.

And while these conversations play inside her head, Jack lies in hospital, pronounced dead.

WHITE, YELLOW AND PURPLE

Lily makes her way to Herbert through the bustle of the city, and when she finally arrives at the park bench, it is two thirty-five. Herbert is asleep beside his meringue nest with its melting lemon cream and his Fedora, still wet with drops left by the rain. And there, on his lap is Jonas's notebook. Lily looks at his face, at his whiskery eyebrows and mottled skin, so old, so wrinkled, so elegant, so right. She is glad to see him.

There are times when Lily feels more like a visiting guest than a permanent resident in the world, but, with Herbert, she feels grounded. She needs this grandfather, this reliable source of affection, she thinks, someone who will always be there, someone who will stay.

She wakes him and kisses his hand, gentle as a butterfly.

'Thank you for waiting, grandpa. I am so glad you did,' she whispers.

Herbert opens his eyes, puts the notebook on the grass, then reaches for her and smiles. His granddaughter's glow reminds him of a rainbow peeping from behind a cloud.

'You are like a rainbow, peeping from behind a cloud,' he says, 'you look so much like your mother.'

Lily buries her face in his shirt, and he puts his arms around her before carefully holding her away as if she were too fragile to hug before exerting a feeble tug to bring her back to him. His arms may be weak, yet he wishes he and Lily could rise and dance, but the music of old age isn't made for dancing.

Before he has a chance to ask why she is late and to wonder whether she knows that descriptions of a young woman very like herself fill the pages of a notebook, Lily tells him about the accident: the seagulls, the sudden rain, the grinding of metal, the mangled bike, the muffled noises, the smell of death.

'Grandpa, I'm scared,' she says.

'I'm not surprised,' answers Herbert, and he stares at the sky for a long while. 'You'll be alright,' he continues, 'You know that I waded fully clothed from the bombing of the beaches of Dunkirk into the safety of the sea. I'm sad that you saw what you saw. It's something you won't forget. But an accident can happen to anyone. When you think of the man who died, try to remember that no story is ever over, not for anyone; there is no final goodbye. The story we think is over is simply a chapter in a longer story we know nothing about, it's simply the end of their share of your story.'

Then they sit for several minutes, but it feels more like an hour; he, thinking about her, and she, thinking about the accident. He is silent and she is silent, but some knowledge passes between them, and a lot is felt in that silence. The only sounds around are the spring breeze, the burbling water of the duckpond and the chatter of house wrens.

Then, as if out of nowhere, Jonas walks towards them, searching for his notebook and his coat.

'Have you seen my notebook and my coat?' he asks. He is polite and softly spoken.

Herbert, who is seldom surprised, sees a young man who could be a character in a novel. Where did he come from? he wonders. He nods, says 'Yes,' and holds out the notebook.

Jonas blushes then sees Lily, Lily and her light.

Just when he thought he knew the story of the rest of his life, there she is.

It is as simple as this; they meet. The girl he has observed running through the park is flesh and blood and sitting on his bench with her grandfather.

This may be nothing. This may be everything. This may be the stranger who touches his heart, this may be the person he has never spoken to but who still makes him feel he has known her all his life.

'What is your name?' he asks, 'I didn't expect to see you on my bench.' She reminds him of someone he can't quite place.

'Why?' she asks.

'It doesn't matter,' he replies.

Lily says, 'Lily,' anyway.

In an inexplicable way, she finds Jonas to be quite different from anyone she has ever met.

'Lily.' He repeats the name because the word delights him. And her voice is as clear as the spring sky.

'Lily of light,' he says, 'your voice will always haunt my soul.' And it feels like he has waited all his life to utter these words.

He closes his eyes at the vision he imagines before him. Jonas, the poet, wants to say, 'Hope flies on unexpected wings. Long before we met, this destiny awaited us,' and 'you smile like an old friend' and more. But because he knows that there are hundreds of different ways of saying one thing, he says nothing. Anyway, truths often lie in words which can't be spoken and even if he could speak, he wouldn't want his truths to be painted all over the park.

So, he simply says, 'My name is Jonas. I am Jonas.'

Jonas looks at Lily like he has found something he lost. He would like this moment to last for ever and he longs to reach out and touch her face, but her light scares him; it has featured so often in his thoughts.

They shake hands but Lily shakes his as if it were a dead flower.

For a moment, Lily and Jonas feel the same warmth and hear the same spring sounds. Just for a moment. Then Jonas sees that the girl in front of him is not the girl in his head because he wasn't dealing with a person, he was dealing with an idea, and one which had more to do with him than with Lily. The girl in his head is a muse who appeared to him along his way, a beacon of light; she was exactly what he wanted her to be. The girl standing before him is just a girl dressed in yellow with a gap between her front teeth and with naive, yellow-brown eyes. She has no idea about a poet's life. He looks at Lily as a man might look at a faded photograph. If he reached out his arms to hold her, she might feel fragile, like paper.

Yet, he can't help himself. 'Everyone has dark and light in them. If we are part of each other's lives, it might be only for this moment when some of your inner dark lifts to allow some of my light to seep into the cracks the darkness leaves behind. Then life will move us on as it must,' he declares.

Lily stands there, watching him and wanting to say 'stop' before the moment unsettles her completely. Then she turns and walks towards Herbert, who bows slightly before saying, 'All love should be taken seriously; leave the young man to believe what he will. But let me take you home now. One of us should talk to your mother, tell her about the accident.'

And just like that the two of them depart – she, dazed, full of disbelief and eager to get away and he, leaning on his stick and with a shuffle in his step because his knee hurts.

'Wait,' cries Jonas, but Lily doesn't. For the rest of her life, she will wonder if she imagined this meeting and will eventually decide she'll never know. For now, she lets Herbert walk her out of the park and the two of them disperse like clouds, leaving Jonas with his notebook, his coat and his broken dreams. And that is that.

At first Jonas is undaunted. He stays on the bench for longer than he planned, the hero of his own love story and as if his heart might soon regain its normal rhythm. He wraps his coat around him, clutches his notebook and smiles as hidden stars do while watching the setting sun.

But then he feels angry and ashamed and, for a fleeting moment, a kind of remorse about his life because he has lost something he never had and because this might be the only kind of loving of which he is capable.

'This is how it ends. You try to tell your story to people who don't know how to listen. It is spring, of course. Every problem in my life takes place in spring,' Jonas explains to a fox which has arrived and is standing beside him like an animal which knows that the sun will set no matter what and that, as far as the sun is concerned, Jonas's problems are as nothing.

'Things don't always work out as planned,' Jonas continues, 'But it may be me. I may have got it wrong. Anyway, my part is over. What to do? Stand up and walk towards whatever is happening next.'

YELLOW AND BLUE

The sun is setting on Monday. Herbert has suggested that Claire and Lily meet in the café where Sasha works. The last of the day's light drifts through the cafe windows, filling every space with its glow. At the same time, Sasha is in her kitchen which is awash with the previous night's handiwork, dealing with the fall-out from the theft and destruction of her car and the first stirrings of a desire to leave London.

Lily arrives early and waits for Claire, who is running late. When Claire does arrive, the first thing Lily sees is blue; a blue scarf, blue eyes – all beautifully blue as if Claire hadn't considered another colour for over sixty years. But Claire's eyes are puffy, and she is wearing more make-up than she wore the previous night. Because she had difficulty finding the café, she looks drawn and flustered.

'Hello Lily,' she says.

'Hello Claire.'

Lily has abandoned any illusions that she and her mother might understand each other. At first, she misinterprets Claire's demeanour for that of a person who would rather be somewhere else, whereas Claire is simply relieved to have made the journey through the café.

A thought strikes Lily: Claire is an ordinary woman just like her and all other women. She has nothing to fear. She stands and lets Claire kiss her cheek, where Claire leaves a lipstick stain.

Then Claire steps back and Lily steps back and sits again only when Claire sits, something her father did.

'Marcus did this,' says Lily, rubbing her cheek.

'Marcus? I didn't notice,' says Claire, who studies her daughter. 'Yellow suits you. I may have said this before; there are times when I look at you and feel I am staring at the sun.'

But Lily's blouse is rumpled, thinks Claire, as if she dressed in a hurry, and Claire can't work out whether Lily wants to be loved or be left alone and whether she is happy or sad.

At first, mother and daughter sit in silence and neither mentions the previous night's encounter. Claire is happy to be here, and Lily, happy to be silent. Their reunion, if you can call it that, thinks Lily, left her feeling disappointed. What more is there to say?

Claire was one of the last people to hear about the accident. When Herbert told her about it, she took the news like a wound. She was sitting in a chair, waiting for her flowers to fold in on themselves for the night. She had decided that, deep down, she and Peter didn't belong to each other. Everything between them must end; his love of her hands, his wish for reassurance, his need, his attempts to please her, her lack of appreciation, the moonlight on their bodies. Everything.

She planned to tell him that something had come up in her life and that she was terribly sorry, or to say, 'Get out. Enough.' And she planned to walk out of the room. Again. Much easier to blame Peter than look at herself.

But this was to be the work of another day.

When Herbert wrapped his arms around her and held her for a long moment, she said, 'I love you, Herbert.'

'I know. I love you, too. Try to move Lily towards forgiveness like an angel moves clouds,' he said.

Now that Claire is in the café, she is simply glad her daughter is unharmed and with her and all she wants to do is keep Lily in her sight. But Lily looks different, and she can't think how. Her daughter's face alters with the slightest breeze of feeling, she thinks. She has thought about Lily every day of her life – every single day – and has missed her with an ache which has been more acute or less; finding her face in the faces of all the young people she met, writing countless letters Lily will never see and hearing an unfamiliar voice she was sure was Lily's.

'I am sorry you saw what you saw this morning,' Claire begins, 'Why didn't you ring me?' Her words sound a little hollow to her, mournful even. She wonders whether to tell Lily she has carried a photograph of her in her wallet for the past thirteen years. It has taken that long to get to this point.

'I tried,' answers Lily, who hardens at the thought of being the object of her mother's pity. If Claire keeps talking, she will have to unpack the memories she keeps in a corner of her mind, so she doesn't cry. A thousand times she has wanted to say, 'I feel like I don't matter to you,' or to ask the question forming once again in her mind, 'How could you leave me to live without you?' but she would be heartless to ask it now. She has lived so long in a world with only a father standing between the known and the unknown. She has lived so long without a mother.

She would also like to say, 'I met a man called Nicholas who made my every day mean something for a while.' She would like to say, 'I am carrying his child. I, too, will be a mother.' But she doesn't realise how difficult it is to say these words until she tries.

She looks at anything – anybody – but her mother. She glances at the cardigan in the basket she brought with her then at her watch, and considers leaving, considers not speaking to Claire again but changes her mind. She has nowhere to go. She needs to decide what she is going to do, what she is going to be. There have been many Mondays in her life. She wonders how this one will end.

Outside the café, life continues. A traffic light changes from red to green, a line of cars marks the start of the late afternoon rush hour, and a breeze rearranges the leaves of a London plane tree lit by the dipping sun. Anyone looking through the window might see a mother and daughter staring at each other as if this were the most ordinary thing to do.

Claire, who is anxious and ever aware of having failed her daughter, reaches for Lily's arm. Her heart is in her hands.

'I am sorry about the accident,' she tries again, 'How can I help?'

And then she continues in a voice full of regret because after more than a decade of estrangement, she has much to say, 'While I might not be able to explain things and while, perhaps, too much time has passed for me to do so, try not to think too badly of me. I would like to help, to say what I'm about to say in such a way that you'll believe me; I would like to say sorry. I am sorry I did this to you.'

Past conversations realign in Lily's head. Why can't her mother keep quiet? Does she have any idea how she sounds? For a moment she hates her mother and comes so close to telling her to stop talking that she feels as if she has. She wants to say, 'Forget about it,' because she tells herself she doesn't care. Instead, she says, 'Oh God, I don't know what to say. What can I say?'

Up to now, Claire and Lily have been speaking in hushed tones, but Claire no longer trusts her voice. She loses her words. She watches them drop to the floor. She shouldn't have said anything, she thinks.

'Here I go again, tripping over my emotions and searching for words,' she says, fumbling in her handbag for a tissue. Her hands are shaking but she is trying to make light of things, to refrain from saying something accusing, like ask Lily why she didn't ring her when she returned to London.

Silence falls again. It seems to spread from the café to the cars waiting on the street outside. A moment passes where the world stands still, and the two women feel a little lost, only their faces say what's in their hearts.

Lily is Lily, thinks Claire. She is twenty-four; old enough to know the damage careless actions can cause, but still so young.

The afternoon slips away. Lily decides to leave. What is she doing here? she wonders. She gathers her basket.

She is always moving, always leaving, never staying, thinks Claire.

But then, for a few minutes, light and dark touch, bathing the cafe in the forgiving, protective light of an early evening, a time when anything might happen. Somewhere in it all, the muted sounds of a clarinet come to them from a radio, filling the empty spaces in the café and bringing with them all the shadows and heartache from the past. Claire shuts her eyes.

A waitress approaches to take their order.

'A weak black tea with a slice of lemon and a scone,' says Claire, 'Will you eat something, Lily? Something? Please sit. Won't you stay?'

Lily looks away from the stories written in the wrinkles around Claire's eyes and mouth to the menu, then back to her mother's face. She replaces her basket on the chair; it would be unkind not to.

She says, 'I'm not hungry, no thank you.'

They wait for Claire's tea to arrive. Nothing seems to move. Then – the last thing Lily expected – the light Jonas left inside her travels through the chinks in her inner dark, and she feels something like compassion rise to the surface. This is a feeling which must have been waiting there all along. She reaches out and touches her mother's hand because there is no reason not to and because she has new life inside her and because after what she saw this morning, she understands that all life is precious and easily broken and that not to take moments of light and understanding is an act of betrayal.

'Oh Claire,' she says as gently as if she were addressing a butterfly, 'Claire, it's ok.'

These may be the most tender words Claire has heard for a long while. Her tears drip on to her hands – the hands which hold her heart. At this moment, she is not at the mercy of her past or the future; all that counts is the here and now. She looks up from her scone to face her daughter and sees the colours of sun and sky.

The sun sets at last. Different lights go on in different cafes and homes all over London and the first pale stars slide into place. Lily puts on her cardigan and Claire wraps her shawl around her. The waitress clears their table, imagining that their meeting comes from years of friendship rather than being the awkward reunion of two people whose feelings are confused. Then she hangs the 'closed' sign on its hook on the door and turns out the lights.

Claire offers to drive Lily home. 'The Mini out there is mine,' she says, but Lily prefers to walk.

'I need the exercise,' she says.

What does her daughter really want? Claire wonders.

When they go their separate ways, Lily in front and Claire a few steps behind, the women pause to look at each other.

'Give me a call,' says Claire, 'or I'll ring you. You know my number.' She gives it to Lily, anyway.

Then she waits a while before driving off, watching Lily walk away with her face turned towards the future, until she is a speck of light in the grey. Lily is almost grown up. But not quite. This much Claire knows. She tells herself that she did what seemed to her to be necessary but needs to give up expecting Lily to see things the way she sees them. She needs to give up hoping Lily will accept the part she played in what is now done. How can she expect Lily to approve of her when she barely approves of herself?

These are the thoughts which run through her mind when she sits in her car. And they will remain with her in the coming days and weeks, appearing while she is plumping cushions, peeling an apple, pondering the arrangement of paintings on a wall or accepting the fact that she may not be able to change as much as she thought she could.

For now, she sends up a prayer to the early evening sky before reapplying her lipstick. Please God, protect Lily; see she is alright. Then she carefully drives away.

Lily walks home deliberately and slowly. She keeps walking without a backward glance but feels less alive, somehow. It occurs to her that the anger she has nursed for so long has been a kind of comfort for being so familiar. She would lose something of her identity if she let it go. A mile passes before she regains her composure.

Later in the year when the wind grows cold, blue skies turn grey and piles of yellow leaves settle on pavements, Claire – when asked, 'what did you say?' and 'what did she say?' – will reply that she doesn't remember exactly. She will say that she doesn't remember how long they spent in the café; it could have been minutes, it could have been hours. She will say that everything moved too quickly and that everything moved too slowly. She will say she is not certain whether Lily needs – or even likes – her but will add, 'We have all the time in the world to work things out; ours is a story without end.'

What Claire will say she is sure of is that she could feel waves of kindness and sympathy washing between them, even if words of that sort weren't spoken – not words she can recall, anyway. She will add that there was nothing else she could do but beg forgiveness.

Lily will keep in her heart her story about walking away from her baby's father just as Claire had done. She will say that there is nothing special about her story except that it is hers. And however little time she and Claire spent in the café and however few words passed between them, she will always remember the afternoon's stillness, the soft leaves of the plane tree and Claire's tired eyes.

GREEN

Sonya was studying her reflection in a kitchen window earlier that Monday, longing for some of Claire's style and beauty and wondering if all she had for comfort was an armful of sunsets. The sisters look alike, in a way, with the beauty of one passing into the plainness of the other. Sonya isn't jealous of Claire but was wondering in a moment of sadness, if she was irredeemably plain despite having been told that her that her eyes light up like leaves in sunshine.

While she was deciding that she preferred afternoons to mornings because she was then sufficiently awake to engage with whatever was happening around her, Jack's brother rang to say he was sorry to bring bad news, but that Jack would not be coming in to help her with the garden. Not this week. Not ever. 'We felt it in our bones at the time,' he said.

Sonya's sadness took her by surprise. Surely death didn't happen on a Monday in spring when she was eating a coconut-date biscuit and drinking coffee? she asked herself. Then the realisation struck that she had lost the man who knew every secret of the apple orchard she planned to plant, the only person she trusted to plant it, and that his passing would leave her with the emptiness which had been her constant companion before they met.

Now, she is sitting in a twilit room, holding a glass of red wine, watching shadows fall like predators and feeling terrible about Jack's accident. His image keeps coming back to her through patterns of light disappearing from the trees outside her window as if spring were ending not beginning. This is a fleeting time of day. Blink and you miss it, she thinks, and this would be a pity because trees sound and smell different in the evening. She remembers all the sunsets she has watched from this lovely window, knowing that she could easily disappear in the shadows of the past if the setting sun didn't bathe her in its daily glow. She has let life slip through her fingers – like shadows – for so long.

She prepares an early supper, feeling loss and indignation. Then the pictures of apple blossom she conjures up in her mind begin to reassure her a little. And the smells of her steaming chicken, mushrooms and brown rice comfort her with the realisation that there are other people around her preparing their suppers in the same way.

And while she will never fully understand why things happen as they do, the great surprise of life in this city is that she is never alone.

BROWN

Peter spent the afternoon in the garage where his father worked trying to salvage what he could of his car and his dignity. Both are destroyed and he can't reach Claire.

'What a Monday it has been. I wish I had stayed in bed,' he said, 'Thank the stars my father didn't live to see this. I wonder what he'd have said?'

Now, he is home. He locks his front door behind him and sits for a long while at the desk in his office, fearing that his heart might collapse. Then he turns his attention from the dust on his desk to the brick wall opposite. All is brown, brown, brown, but splashed, at least, with flecks of gold which bring individual bricks to life. He moves from his desk to the window where the sight of a distant plane tree holding the first leaves of spring makes him yearn for home. Wherever that is.

He needs to take the night off, have a glass of wine, watch television, make his bed, and go to sleep early.

And do something about the heaviness which has settled on his chest.

There is a knock on his door, then keys turn in his lock.

When Claire walks into the room, Peter's face is white.

'Shall I take your shawl?' he manages to ask.

WHITE

Morning has turned to afternoon and afternoon to evening. Herbert is sitting outside his house once again, looking at the sky and telling the early stars his stories and, in turn, listening to theirs. His fedora is beside him, of course, because he can't do anything without it; it reminds him of who he is.

Now, he is eating a just-baked honey and oat flapjack and thinking about life and love and about the fact that both keep changing. He feels lucky to have loved two women and he thinks about his Annettes and about his betrayal of the first. He thinks about the ways in which one human being can mean so much, and then, so little. He never understands why things happen to some people and not to others. Destiny is made so accidentally. He wonders if it is because of his decisions that neither daughter has yet found love.

Now he watches the sky turn from white to yellow to pink to purple and the city light up against the night as if it were watching him back. His house is quiet with the slightly sad hush he expects at this time of night. Sonya and Claire are only as different from each other as green is from blue, he thinks, and some of the same blood flows through them. His pride in them will never diminish even if it takes years till their tasks are done or until they work each other out.

But people must decide how best to live their own lives. And this he knows as surely as he knows that days pass too quickly, that twilights linger and that the night stays.

If he is feeling pride and gratitude for all he has achieved, he is also feeling wistful. Why would he not feel this way? There will be sunsets he will not live to see, and he won't always be around to hear branches tapping against his windows or the squawks of seagulls headed for parks, or to smell the comforting scent of almond biscuits or savour steaming cups of tea.

If he has loved and lost and loved and lost again, he did this with a heart so big, he thought he could change the world. But when his wives died, each in her time, his living stopped, and all he could do was count clouds. Still, the Annettes continue to live beside him, and each is rooted in his soul. He often pictures them, sitting under the stars, listening while he tells them that he has become an old man, and explaining how long and surprisingly cold spring nights can be.

'If my escape from Dunkirk defines me, if I live in the past,' he tells a wren looking for a place to roost for the night, 'So be it. And I need not trouble my daughters with needless regrets or memories I would rather forget. Instead, I shall let them know that ordinary life is the most precious thing they will ever experience. That is all.'

He glances at his wristwatch. It is eight thirty, neither day nor night. He stands slowly and pushes his glasses up his nose. Time to bid goodnight to the sky, go inside, bake a cake, perhaps, and close the door on Monday.

PURPLE

The warm, blossom-scented air of April swirls around Jonas who decides to spend another night on the bench he thinks of as his own. The only way to understand a bench is to sleep on it, he muses, and a man who sleeps draped only in purple sky on a lonely bench, can be as brave as any.

He takes off his shoes and stretches out on the bench which feels tailored to his body and his lips move in time to new poems forming in his head.

PINK

There is all manner of restlessness in houses and streets in the city this Monday night. Claire changed her mind about returning home from the cafe and has driven, instead, towards Peter; Jonas is awake on his bench, but the night keeps pushing him back, Lily is walking her dark way home, lost in thoughts about Nicholas; Sonya is struggling with solitary plans to plant her apple orchard; Herbert's pineapple upside-down cake is waiting too long to come out of the oven, and the moon which is shining on Sasha's birthday, keeps disappearing behind clouds.

Sasha sits by an open window in her freshly painted kitchen until the light outside disappears completely and the walls' pinkness blends with the dark. Here she is, wearing a headscarf and waiting in silence, like the silence before music plays, and licking cream cheese icing off her fingers. She is not thinking about her car – she doesn't care for cars and has no use for them –and she is not thinking about tomorrow, but still, her future stirs like seeds under the soil in the pots on her patio.

Sasha is afraid. She is afraid she will become music no-one hears or a book no-one reads. She turns her mind to Lithuania, the country of her parents' birth, a place of fields and rivers, a country which defines her whether she likes this or not. She is thinking that if she were to go there, she might be reunited with Darius because she has heard that the dead shelter the living. She is also thinking that she might change her name to Alice.

BLUE AND BROWN

'I feel tired,' Claire tells Peter, 'Very tired.' She also feels exposed and out of control. She has been crying and doesn't notice, at first, that Peter is pale and distracted.

She traces her beautiful hands with their oval-shaped nails along the back of a chair, hoping to attract his attention.

Peter looks at her and a strangely comforting thought trickles through him; because he has little left, he has little to lose and little reason to be concerned about losing any more. But this doesn't stop him worrying about what Claire thinks of him or about what she will say.

He mops her flushed face with a tissue then reaches for her satiny hands. Like peaches, he thinks. And there he was believing he was a man who disliked tears. But there is something about her he can't put his finger on. Should he put on music? Should he ask her to dance? What can he do to make her happy?

'Oh sweetheart,' he says because she touches his heart. 'I am here. You can cry with me. I don't care if you need to stay up crying all night long.' But as soon as he says this, he thinks this was the wrong thing to say.

'Really?' she asks, then with an uncharacteristic loss of control, starts crying all over again.

'Yes,' he replies. As easy as that.

He wants to add, 'We've made it this far, don't leave me' and thinks, as he so often does, that she is the most beautiful woman he has seen. Now, he leans his head towards her and says, 'Whatever happens tomorrow, we have tonight.'

And they plan to go on together to Tuesday and beyond.

Peter chooses to say nothing about his day because, for all he knows, she may be going through hell, and he wants to help her. Anyway, he wouldn't want her to hear him ranting about a car.

What would Kirk Douglas do now? he wonders.

'You smell of spring,' he says, 'I'll hold you in my arms till your life rights itself and you feel you can carry on.'

'You can't mean that,' she says. But he does.

He strokes her face, trying to ignore the faraway look in her eyes. It's as if she were envisioning a life somewhere beyond his walls, he reflects, a life which doesn't include him. No matter how well he thinks he knows her, he fears he never will.

'Look at me, Claire,' he says, 'please.'

Still, he feels gratitude. He reminds himself how lucky he is to have met her even if he doesn't say so; it might not help right now. Anyway, an end can happen at any time. You get used to someone and they leave. Everyone leaves, he thinks. He has learnt how to let go.

Claire slips home before ten because she is as restless as her daughter and because she feels in danger of being misunderstood. She tells Peter that she needs a night's sleep.

While driving home and listening to 'Meet Me Halfway' by the Black-Eyed Peas on the radio, she wonders how she can be a mother when she can barely tolerate being a lover.

Peter closes his front door. What do he and Claire have beside each other? he thinks – and they may not even have that.

He plans to ring his sister as soon as the first clouds of dawn come floating into the sky. He cares what she thinks and will try to save the situation between them with a joke, perhaps. Family is family, and tomorrow is tomorrow. Then he turns on the television and watches the news; good or bad, news changes every day, he reflects.

PINK AND YELLOW

The moon has reappeared and is shining its light on Sasha who is standing at her sink, finishing the dishes. She is thinking that the day has passed as well as it can and has changed into comfortable pyjamas under her apron. Her half-eaten cupcake with its unlit candle sits melting on the table and a slight smell of paint still lingers on the walls. Because the glow from the outside passage peeps through the gap at the bottom of her front door, she opens it and peers into the hallway. Outside the building, it's one of those nights when she fears the city might swallow her if she were to leave her home. Then she sees Lily, who has been out walking, and is now shining her light up the staircase.

'Won't you come in, Lily?' she asks because she knows who she is, 'It's my thirty-ninth birthday. I like your name, by the way. Mine is Sasha, but I'd prefer to have been called Alice.'

'Are you sure?' asks Lily, who hesitates before walking through Sasha's door, 'Happy birthday.'

Sasha wipes her hands on her apron which she then removes and relights her birthday candle. She has no shoes on and the strawberry mark on her neck seems to glow.

Until now, she and Lily have been strangers, but on a night like this, she would like to take a stranger into her home and make her a friend.

'I'm sorry about your car,' says Lily, glancing at the ornaments dotted around, and at photographs of Darius seated behind a wheel. 'Crazy world. Who would do such a thing?'

Sasha shrugs. 'Oh, that's all right, I'll deal with it,' she says because she thinks it's just a car. She offers coffee and a share of the cupcake; 'it's all I have to offer right now,' she says, and they sit at her kitchen table, stirring their drinks and staring at the walls.

'Tell me about yourself,' Sasha suggests because she wants to know.

Then, it could be because of the flickering birthday candle or because the room's pink other-worldliness moves through her or because she can't help herself or because there is something about Sasha which makes her want to confide, that Lily says straight away, 'I am expecting a child. No-one else knows – there is no-one else to tell.'

Sasha feels an emptiness at the pit of her stomach which isn't hunger. She nibbles at her share of cupcake. 'Oh Lily, that's sad. How long have you been keeping this to yourself?' she asks. She hasn't considered having a child and she may not have a child, but she sometimes wonders what she is missing.

'Three or four weeks,' Lily answers.

Lily goes on to talk without stopping about Cyprus and about the night her old life ended. About Nicholas, the child's father; says he works in her father's pharmacy and that she never thought she would meet a man like him. About the fact that she sometimes goes a whole day without wondering what he is doing. About growing up with only a father for company and comfort, about not being able to confide in Claire and that this makes her feel almost constantly unhappy.

'But this may not be of interest,' she suggests.

'Yes, it is,' answers Sasha, nodding her head.

'What about your life?' Lily asks, sitting forward.

'Mine?' Sasha replies.

Sasha explains how her mother died. She talks about Lithuania with its forest and lakes. About the birds which flock to her patio at sunrise. About the hydrangeas seen through the window, which catch the light of the moon. About having attended music college and about wanting to be a singer but having to work part-time as a waitress. About Darius leaving.

'Why?' Lily asks.

'It just happened that way,' Sasha replies. 'Didn't you think it strange that your mother would leave you?'

'She'd had a hard life; I don't think she knew what else to do,' replies Lily, looking once again at the photographs of Sasha's parents displayed around the room.

Both Lily and Sasha are only children, and both need to talk. For the moment, this unites them. They listen and talk and talk and listen. They talk of the past then look to the future. They take turns discussing their plans or the want of them, for both are on the cusp. They say they hope to keep going, to live their lives even if time passes and choices narrow. And while they sit with their cups of coffee, the moon disappears again behind a cloud.

'Will you keep your baby?' Sasha asks, 'Does Nicholas know? Will you share your story with your mother, or will you risk losing her all over again?'

Sasha's questions settle somewhere outside Lily's head. She touches her stomach. 'I'm not sure if that's possible. I don't know if I can – share my story, I mean. Will you go to Lithuania as your father did?'

'Yes,' answers Sasha, 'I plan to write a letter to the owner of the café, explaining my intention to pack my bags and leave because there are times when people have to get away. I shall say that I know Lithuania's wheatfields and horses and pink houses standing between hedges are calling me. And I shall tell anyone who asks, that I want to be someone with a future not just a past; someone defined by the love I hope to gain, not the loves I have lost.'

She goes on to say that when she arrives in Lithuania, she hopes to live an ordinary life or perhaps she'll try painting patterns such as a bird might make if you dipped its wings in paint then set them loose on paper. 'I may even buy a car,' she declares, 'I can fit in there or anywhere because I am a singer, I know how to perform.'

'You can always return to London,' says Lily, rearranging her hair in its clasp.

'I don't know,' replies Sasha, although as she says the words, it becomes clear to her that she won't.

'I may return to Cyprus,' says Lily, 'because you never know.'

'You can't mean that,' says Sasha who looks at Lily and sees that she could.

They continue talking as if they were old friends until Lily announces that she must leave in a voice more abrupt than she intends. It's nine-forty. She never stays long. She takes Sasha's hand. 'I must go,' she says, 'And thank you. I'm glad we spoke.'

'Take care of yourself,' says Sasha, who hears what people say as well as what they don't. 'This must be difficult for you. I'm sorry.'

Lily nearly cries but doesn't let herself. 'I'll be fine,' she says, 'Thank you, again, Sasha. Goodbye.'

'Goodbye Lily. Thank you.'

Then the women separate as hastily as they reached out and Lily walks away like the moving bloom she is. There's little point saying, 'Let's meet again,' thinks Sasha; so be it.

She returns to staring out of her window; a shift in the clouds reveals the moon, which was there all along, of course and the stars are shining like blossom. She pictures her mother standing on her patio, draped in a shawl and watching the sun rise on her future, reminding her that her spirit lives on in birds. Lily's words linger in the room and Sasha sits for a long while thinking about them. Did anything she said get through to the younger woman? It's not that Lily should have to listen to her, but Lily seemed unreal and unaware, somehow, like a child or a person living a lie or a dream. But that's how it is for some people, muses Sasha.

What Sasha can't know is that she has a big life ahead. When the future opens, fame will find her and she will become known as the singer named Alice, who sings like a bird. For now, she wonders how she could have imagined she was the only one who wasted love on people who don't deserve it.

Lily feels lighter. She crosses the landing and opens her front door, feeling glad that the day is over even if it isn't over everywhere because Herbert is baking, Jonas is fighting sleep, and Claire and Peter are wondering separately where to go from here. The creatures of the night have work to do, and stars are on the move.

Sasha is kind, thinks Lily, who has no idea how hard Sasha was trying.

And two coffee cups and crumbs from a birthday cupcake sit on a tray next to the sink in Sasha's kitchen, catching the moon's light before it disappears once again behind clouds.

WHITE

Herbert bakes when he worries; he bakes when he worries about Claire. It troubles him that he might have failed her. Does she lack courage? He wishes he hadn't passed some of his struggles to her.

But Herbert also bakes because a good cake makes him feel that he is creating joy from his fingertips. He can still picture the muscles in his mother's arms sifting flour and wielding a rolling pin and he finds nothing as calming as measuring and mixing.

Tonight, he is on the point of taking his pineapple upside-down cake out of the oven when his mind travels back to Dunkirk. His mind weighs up the past like a cake, it feels comfortable in Dunkirk and his days and nights are full of dreaming because his memories of Dunkirk keep him going.

He will never forget Robert, his friend killed by a bomb dropped on to the beach where they were standing, or the feel of the sea seeping through his socks under the light of the moon – which is the same no matter which sky you are standing under, he muses. A comforting thought.

He looks at his wristwatch. It continues to keep good time if he remembers to wind it. It is ten- to-ten and there in the oven is his waiting cake. He stretches out to remove thc cake but loses his balance. He tries to steady himself on the kitchen table, but his legs give way, and he falls. One minute he is standing and the next, he is on the floor.

Herbert checks himself; he is not injured, nothing is broken, his glasses are still where they should be, and he can see. He isn't scared of falling, as such. After all these years, he has become increasingly unsteady and has fallen many times and most of what he has learnt he has learnt from falling. But falling to the ground with no-one there to catch him hurts, and he can't bring himself to get up. Before he can stop them, tears flow. They slip down his face and onto his mouth. They flow from his cheeks to his shoes. They flow because his knees crack painfully, they flow for his friend, Robert, they flow because his cake will burn and because baking suddenly feels strangely unsatisfying, they flow because he aches with a weariness he has not noticed before and they flow because wherever he turns, he sees pictures of his wives.

Herbert wipes his tears with his handkerchief and when they subside, he feels himself again. It's not possible to live without losing something now and again, he thinks, and one burnt cake makes room for future baking. Because he lacks the strength in his arms to pull himself up - even with his stick, he shuffles along the floor, inch by inch, till he reaches a wall. He leans against it and reaches for his Fedora which he puts on his head.

BROWN AND WHITE

Peter is uneasy. Claire's departure has left him troubled, and it's too early to sleep. When he felt like this on previous occasions, he drove around London, leaving his neighbourhood to watch the wanderers and creatures of the gloom come out in the dark like night lilies. Now, he has no car, so he puts mints in his pocket and decides to walk. He has questions to mull over. He'll be home by midnight.

The night is as quiet as it's going to get. Small clouds drift through the sky. Everything is strange but everything is familiar and most of the people walking are those who can't sleep or are haunted by lost love or are hoping to slip unnoticed through the shadows. And any of these people think Peter is one of them. He wanders around aimlessly, following the night's small noises, looking in lighted windows at families talking or dining, passing unlit houses where people lie sleeping with their hopes and their mistakes, and observing quivering trees and cars standing idle.

On nights like this, you question things you ordinarily wouldn't, and end up in places you ordinarily wouldn't, and before he can say 'life is life', he has walked almost three miles to a house near the King's Road; the house is Herbert's, and he knows this because Claire pointed it out to him. He can't think what brought him to this point, and, in the future, will wonder how long he'd been hatching this without being aware, but now that he is here, he finds he has a plan.

From the street, Herbert's kitchen looks dark. The only lights inside come from the oven, a lamp which gives the room a solemn glow, and a stray moonbeam which shines on Herbert's face. Peter sees Herbert on the floor and is so shocked, at first, that all he can do is stare. Then he knocks on the window. 'I am Peter, Claire's friend,' he mouths, 'May I come in?' and he surprises himself with his question.

'Push the door. It's open,' answers Herbert. He needs help so invites Peter in as if he expected him all along. Although they haven't met, the men have heard about each other, and each is entwined with Claire.

Peter enters the kitchen and sees Herbert half propped against a wall and half splayed on the floor. He looks as pale as the moon, thinks Peter, but as tough and still as an oak.

Peter stumbles back a step, then pauses for a couple of moments, not sure what to do. He should say something but can't find words. He needs a cigarette.

'Are you alright?' he asks, full of concern for the older man.

Herbert sits still, not moving, with his Fedora perched on his head. Then he raises his hand and says, 'I am Herbert, Claire's father,' aware that Peter knows. 'Don't be alarmed; my fall took no time but has left me stretched out on the floor and I haven't yet found a way to get up.'

'I am Peter,' Peter repeats, 'Claire's friend. I am sorry, I know it's late. I am sorry to see you like this.'

'It happens,' says Herbert who doesn't ask, 'What brought you here?' Instead, he asks, 'How are you?'

'I'm good. I'm good,' Peter answers, 'How long have you been on the floor?'

'I don't know,' says Herbert, 'not long – and I am fine.'

Peter looks around the plain kitchen with its white walls and shining surfaces and at the row of hyacinths in pots on the windowsill. He studies Herbert in the gloom which surrounds them.

Herbert points to the oven. 'Would you mind rescuing my cake?' he asks.

Peter removes the burnt cake from the oven as if this were the most ordinary thing in the world to do and puts it on the table together with his worry beads and bifocals. Then, he crouches in the shadows beside Herbert, hoping that it's not too dark for Herbert to see him. His body twinges as if he had walked much further than he did. What does Herbert think of him? He so wants Herbert to look at him and approve.

'What a night,' he says.

They shake hands and Peter keeps hold of Herbert's hand, which is elegant, he thinks, with long fingers and protruding veins. They are each of them alone, the room is barely lit, and he can't help himself. This may seem a little unusual, but what else can he do? muses Peter.

'Would you like a mint?' he asks.

'No thank you,' Herbert answers.

Herbert glances at Peter whose profile he can just make out. Peter is around fifty, handsome and polite but tired and troubled looking, with a whiff of cigarette on his minty breath, and not what he expected. Both men are widowers but are ageing differently; one, hoping for a future, the other settled in his past. If Peter is the man for his daughter, thinks Herbert, he is going with it, but he needs to understand more.

'Is there a problem?' he asks. People have secrets you can't imagine, and Peter strikes him as a man whose life hasn't always gone well.

'I live with an almost continuous sense of failure,' Peter hears himself say.

'Why?' Herbert asks.

Then Peter shares the part of his story they have in common; the part which brought him here, the part called Claire.

'I will never understand the hurt Claire feels or why she cries,' he says.

Herbert isn't sure how to respond. He could say he knows about the pain Claire feels. He knows she needs to cry. He could say he has known love and known it twice. He could say that love is the only thing which matters and tell Peter to enjoy what he has while he has it. Instead, he says, 'Some of my choices may have made things complicated for Claire. What led you to her?'

Peter doesn't answer. He isn't surprised to hear what Herbert says but decides not to share stories about brief and unsatisfactory love affairs which have remained unspoken for years. He directs Herbert a look of gratitude and nods his head, 'I know what you mean.'

Then the men sit in silence, aware of the impossibility of each picturing the other at his best right now and both feeling the awkwardness of strangers. A shyness comes over Peter; it appears he has nothing more to say.

Can strangers really know what to do with or for each other? wonders Herbert, who feels increasingly uncomfortable and wants Peter to leave.

When Hebert says he is ready, Peter helps him to his feet and hands him his stick, wondering if it's impolite to abandon him, having witnessed something so personal and not meant to be seen. 'Shall I take you to your bed? Will you be alright?' he asks.

Herbert raises a hand to indicate no help needed and that he'll be alright, and finds he is filled with sudden tenderness for the younger man.

'Are you sure?' asks Peter. He gathers his worry beads and bifocals and makes his way to the front door.

Herbert leans against his kitchen table and waves. He opens his mouth then closes it; he isn't one for talk these days. There is more he could say, but not tonight; he is tired and further words are best avoided.

'Goodbye,' he says, 'And don't give up. We all struggle with things we don't understand, and you are more helpful to Claire than you realise.'

'Thank you,' Peter says.

'Don't mention it,' says Herbert.

Peter pauses for a moment, then closes the front door and turns to go and does so quickly because the familiar aching pressure has returned to his chest.

Herbert waits till he hears his front gate click shut. Through his kitchen window, he sees Peter's thickset figure disappearing around the corner and the night closing over him like a flower. Herbert smooths his hair and tucks in his shirt till almost no trace remains of his dishevelled self; even his kitchen seems to sink back to normal. Then he walks to his bedroom, leaning on his stick, taking with him his Fedora, and trying to work out how he could possibly have fallen – but he did. Living alone demands a precise assessment of time. He checks his watch. Forty minutes have passed. Before talking off his clothes, he spends a moment or two telling the Annettes in his head what happened in his kitchen; 'hard to believe,' he says. Then he gets into bed and folds his arms over his chest as is his custom. It will soon be tomorrow and there is a cake on his table, waiting a decision.

On his way home, Peter passes the same quiet houses with their sleeping people, feeling not quite sure what he feels. At first, he has trouble believing what has taken place, but by the time he reaches his small house, he feels better – 'normal' he tells himself; his chest has eased, and he is buoyed by ideas forming in his mind which have more to do with carrying on than with giving up. He plans to visit Claire. Although the details of his visit to Herbert will remain his secret, he will explain how they met. He will say that she has the most beautiful hands he has ever seen. He will ask her to help him love her, say that he doesn't require her to change for him to love her and that they should try to work things out before it's too late and before his heart gives in. He will add that never in his life could he have imagined a woman like her would choose him. He will also say that he would like to dance with her like no-one is watching. 'I, too, can dance,' he will say.

In the future, they will be in and out of each other's lives because a delicate web of need surrounds them and because loving someone means that you keep taking them back.

For now, he has a shower and washes off the night. Then he hangs a green shirt and tie over his brown suit for tomorrow because tomorrow is another day.

GREEN

It is ten forty. Sonya is lying between sheets and under a blanket in her darkened bedroom, which is now lit only by a bedside lamp. She is thinking that she may not be as different from her neighbours as she fears. She is also thinking that there is something about lying alone in bed with the dark outside the window which reminds her that life doesn't always work out as planned.

Her thoughts turn to Herbert, as they do so often, and to the mother she loved and the sunny afternoons they spent in the countryside with leaves in their hair, and inventing names for secret flowers. Now, the woman she has become yearns to recapture just one of those sunny afternoons because she thinks she has lost her way.

She stares at a photograph she keeps on the table beside her bed. In it, she is standing behind Claire who, like Lily in a photograph taken much later, is seated, smiling and looking straight to camera, while Sonya is tucked into shadows and looking down. How plain she looked, even then, she thinks, and how lacking in light compared with Claire's confident glow.

Claire is seven years older and lives in a world which doesn't include her, she muses. She often mourns Claire as if her half-sister were dead. But even if they have little to say to each other, she knows their roots will always be tangled and that the time has come for her to invite Claire into her garden for tea.

In her mind she imagines them sitting on wicker chairs, chatting as sisters should – sisters who listen and don't judge. They talk about apples and about Jack and about the apple trees he couldn't plant. She serves an apple pie, displayed on a cake stand with whipped cream on the side, and she offers this with whatever emotions arise. There are also chocolate brownies and cheese scones, unsalted butter and her plum jam to enjoy, and she is wearing lipstick and her best green dress to show she has emerged from Claire's shade.

She won't say, 'We have nothing in common' or 'Apples aren't always sweet' or 'Green is the colour of envy' or 'No-one can escape the shadows family cast.' Instead, she will say, 'There is someone in this world who longs for your friendship. Let green heal what it can. How do people get through life without sisters? If you have a sister, broken hearts mend.'

Then the two of them will swap stories before it's too late and before they forget. They will talk about Herbert.

Sonya will say, 'The father we share walked beside me like I was a fairy.'

'The father we share is a stranger to me,' Claire will say, 'He wasn't the best father, but he was my father, and his faults and failures mean nothing to me now.'

Sonya will continue, 'At least I have a home which protects me.'

And Claire will smile and say, 'Home is neither here nor there. Home isn't a place, it's a person. There is little point looking back on your life, wondering why things turned out the way they did – this is not a time to pretend you're just a woman standing in shadow. You are more than that; you are a sister.'

Sonya will reply, 'The coffee is hot. This cup is yours.' And she will think that things are exactly as they should be. She has a sister who loves her, and home is where her sister is.

Now, before falling asleep, Sonya decides to send Claire a hand-written letter on cream-coloured notepaper edged with green, requesting the pleasure of her company for tea. She leaves her window open to the night because she loves the smell of the garden and feels the need of its air. Soothed by her resolve, she surrenders to shadows cast by the apple-coloured moon, feeling happy for the first time in ages.

At the same moment, but in a house not far from the King's Road, Herbert is lying on his bed, with his Fedora on the pillow next to his and is planning to ring Sonya in the morning. He wishes to explain that while he is aware that she knows about Claire's old life, Claire has changed. He also wishes to say that he is as fragile as spring blossom and is not long for this world, and that his daughters should make contact before it is too late. Then, it's as if his thoughts wing their way across the city and enter Sonya's house through her open bedroom window.

Father and daughter sleep. And while they do, endings and beginnings follow on from one another as the earth turns around the sun.

PURPLE

It is quarter to eleven as far as he knows. Jonas, who senses time even when he doesn't know it exactly, puts his shoes under the bench. His unread notebook lies beside him on the grass.

There is no-one about except the fox. He, too, feels the night's breezes. He, too, thinks of the bench as his own.

Jonas tells the fox, 'I will never lose my love for this city, but its people don't stay with me; they leave. So, I must keep moving – it's a choice I make. I still have a pocketful of dignity and my next story will find me. It always does.'

Then he raises his hand as if pointing to a spot in the air which marks his next destination. 'My bench no longer beckons; it's as if it knows I am about to leave. I shall hand it over to you. And, you never know, a page of my unread poetry may be lifted by the wind, blown over rooftops, land in a room or garden and mean something to the person who reads it. You never know.'

The fox cocks its head as if to say, 'I'll be pleased to hear a poem of yours. You are a wanderer and a poet. Take care of yourself. Enjoy the rest of your journey. Your story will one day sprout beautiful tendrils you can't know about now, because, for the moment, they are coiling out of sight.'

Then Jonas will go off in search of the perfect love he imagines only in the privacy of his heart because if love is available, he'll choose it. He will leave the photograph of the cyclist to his room's next occupant – as he must, as well as the newspapers he collects, but he will leave nothing of himself. He will fall in love with autumn all over again and make the long walk out of London when green leaves turn yellow and blue skies grey. This is his destiny and autumn is his season. April's pink and white mean nothing to him. And Lily – more the sense of her than the person – will accompany him.

After he has gone, life in London will continue to tick by in streets and on pavements, in houses and apartments, in beds and around dining tables and in dreams and prayers. People will keep going as they always have because that's life and because London is a city of infinite possibility. This doesn't mean Jonas won't be missed, of course. He is an integral part of the neighbourhood.

There will come a day when he'll look up and realise he hasn't wandered off in a long time and he'll know he is home. For now, he decides not to think of himself as a rootless man. Instead, he will consider himself blessed because life offered him the chance if only for a few moments, of sharing Lily's light.

A peacock which has escaped from the park zoo cries out from a treetop under the moon. Jonas laughs as if there were people around to hear him. He is glad to begin again, to walk forward to new places and new houses, or backwards to familiar places. He knows how to do both. He has done both before.

YELLOW

It is eleven-thirty-three according to the clock on the wall in Lily's flat near Battersea Park. Lily is sitting on her kitchen floor, with the palms of her hands on her stomach, bare under her pyjamas. She is wondering at the steps or missteps which have led her to this point, and she is frightened. She has spent so long living her life for other people.

She gets up and walks to the window. She lets the moon caress her shoulders with its gentle light. If she were to lean out, she might see an empty park bench lit by stars. If she were to stretch out further, she might spot Peter's back disappearing through his front door. And there in the distance is the River Thames, winding its way through the city. There are times when Lily feels like flotsam begin swept along by water, just drifting along and not thinking.

YELLOW AND BLUE

At ten minutes before midnight in Bloomsbury, Claire is waiting for the kettle to boil.

She looks out at the view across to St. Pancras and King's Cross Stations and at the dark blue sky. Nights, she decides, can bring comfort because they carry with them the promise of opportunities, feelings, possibilities. There will be moments in the future when her life will feel like it is beginning anew; moments when she will see life as a gift and understand that this life, her only possible life, is the one she has been waiting for all along.

Now, she stops taking in the view and starts picturing Lily, standing in her kitchen, perhaps, or seated on the floor.

Lily decides to ring her mother. Before dialling Claire's number, she plans what she is going to say. Talking with Claire on the telephone will be best, she thinks, because she won't have to sit across from her or eat food she doesn't like or deal with the worry etched on Claire's face.

The soft ring of the phone splinters the silence of Claire's orderly apartment. It also gives her a start because soft rings sound loud in the dark and because a ringing phone around midnight seldom augurs well.

Claire puts a spoonful of honey in her tea. London honey tastes unlike honey from anywhere else, she thinks. Because she is mulling this over, and because she is always slightly surprised that anyone should call her at all, she looks at her phone, has a sip of tea then answers on the fifth ring.

'It's Lily. Thank God you answered,' says Lily, 'Sorry to ring at this time. Were you waiting?'

'Lily?' Claire asks, 'Where are you? Where are you?' And she asks this twice because Lily's voice sounds too close, as if she were speaking from the next room. Although she had been wondering whether Lily might ring, the call right now feels like an interruption; it comes at a time when she is feeling safe and alone. Still, she continues, 'It's good to hear your voice. I was thinking of you. How are you?'

Because she is tired, she imagines her voice being tangled with Lily's somewhere in the wires. Phone calls with their false expectations, bring intrusion into order, she thinks.

'I am in my flat,' says Lily, who is looking at the colours of the night. 'Everything is fine.'

'Everything?' asks Claire, who takes another sip of tea. 'I feel like a part of you is somewhere else.'

Silence floats through the air waves then Lily hears the faint sound of voices followed by a window closing. All she can think is, please Claire, don't hang up. She waits till Claire's voice comes back on the line then says again, 'Sorry to call so late. Are you still there? Is Peter with you?' because she never knows.

'I'm right here,' says Claire, 'I'm not going anywhere, and Peter is not with me. Could you speak a little louder? I'm struggling to hear you.' Claire presses the phone to her ear. 'Is something wrong?' she asks because she is fearful of what Lily is about to say and because asking if something is wrong is what she does. Still, does anyone know anything about anything? she asks herself.

Lily has been thinking that she might collect her belongings and leave London if she can't find work or if the challenges of her life in the city become too difficult. She pictures herself returning to Cyprus. She toys with the possibility of returning – with a daughter, perhaps? – to Nicholas because she has a sense of his life all the time. She might even marry him if he'll have her. But she has run away once. Can she do it again? Claire looms close. Even when they were miles from each other, it was the same. A stream of pity flows through her for them both; her loyalty to Claire is more profound than she realises. If she leaves again, she will always be staying.

'I simply wanted to know that you were there,' Lily says more softly than usual and as if she were being overheard. 'Sorry,' she adds because Claire's awkwardness is palpable even over the phone; her breathing is quicker, and she sounds as uncertain as Lily feels.

Telephone conversations are so inadequate, so lacking in gesture or expression, thinks Claire, it is so easy to say the wrong thing. She is smiling, but if, on the other hand, she was to cry she would at least be spared the indignity of crying in view of anyone.

'Sorry for what?' she asks, 'Nothing to be sorry about. I'm glad to hear from you – to hear your voice. I thought you might ring. Can't you sleep?'

'I'm ok,' answers Lily. 'I'm not tired.' She stares at the moon.

'I'm pleased to hear it,' answers Claire, who feels tired with a tiredness she hasn't known for months. 'It's been a long day.'

She wraps her silk dressing gown around her and returns to picturing Lily; her curly hair, pale skin, yellow-brown eyes, gap-toothed smile and her voice which is so at odds with her radiance. Is she wearing her yellow pyjamas?

They have got this far, she thinks, and at least they are talking. But it will all take time; things which happen in childhood don't go away. She can't turn herself into a different woman, but she can change what she hopes for – what she expects. And no matter what they are wearing, they can control how they sound over the phone. Still, she can't get away from fearing that one day she'll be sitting at home, drinking tea with lemon and looking at the sky, when someone will ring and tell her that Lily has gone.

Midnight strikes. Lily looks at the clock on her wall. Outside the window, Venus shines its light on to London's spring landscape – a landscape both vast and intimate, which holds in its heart the souls of all the people who have ever walked through it. Monday becomes Tuesday – a day which begins like any other day until unexpected snow flurries fall, a cream-coloured envelope edged with green finds its way to Claire's door, a just-baked ginger cake gleams on a kitchen table in a house near the King's Road, and new stories emerge.

The phone lines crackle with words left unsaid as mother and daughter fall back into silence. Then – it may be because she can't see Claire or because she is frightened and can't come up with a plan – a voice Lily barely recognizes as her own winds its way like a ribbon through Herbert's assurance that no story is ever over and says, 'Claire, I have something to tell you.'

ACKNOWLEDGEMENT

Thank you to my husband, David, for his support and to Shelley Weiner for being my mentor.